A Place between Stations

A PLACE BETWEEN STATIONS

Stories by
Stephanie Allen

University of Missouri Press
Columbia and London

Copyright © 2003 by Stephanie Allen
University of Missouri Press, Columbia, Missouri 65201
Printed and bound in the United States of America
All rights reserved
5 4 3 2 1   07 06 05 04 03

Library of Congress Cataloging-in-Publication Data

Allen, Stephanie, 1962–
  A place between stations : stories / by Stephanie Allen.
      p. cm.
  ISBN 0-8262-1444-4 (alk. paper)
  I. Title.
  PS3601.L436 P56 2003
  813'.6—dc21

                                    2002014508

⊗™ This paper meets the requirements of the
American National Standard for Permanence of Paper
for Printed Library Materials, Z39.48, 1984.

    Design and Composition: Stephanie Foley
    Cover design: Jennifer Cropp
    Printer and binder: The Maple-Vail Book Manufacturing Group
    Typefaces: Palatino and Spumoni

"A Place between Stations" first appeared in *Water~Stone*, vol. 1, no. 1 (Fall
1998). "Carved in Vinyl" first appeared in *The Madison Papers*, vol. 1, no. 1
(Fall/Winter 2000). "Souvenir" is reprinted from *The Massachusetts Review*, vol.
42, no. 3 (Autumn 2001). "Marisol's Things" is reprinted from *The BlackWater
Review*, vol. 5 (2000/2002). "Keep Looking" is reprinted from *The Connecticut
Review*, vol. 25, no. 1 (Spring 2003).

For Gerald Kenneth Allen and Elizabeth Foster Allen,
my parents

CONTENTS

A Place between Stations

CARVED IN VINYL

People say the suburbs are regimental, all the houses cut to the same pattern, the siding monotonous, the lawns perfect. But when we moved out of the city, Robert and I and the kids, what bothered me was that there were no sidewalks, and for quite a long time I felt lost. The lawn spilled right out into the road; there was nowhere to stroll. I fretted about raising the children in a place where something so elemental was lacking. They'd miss out on hopscotch, real hopscotch, the kind where the measure of the squares was the depth of a concrete slab, nothing more and nothing less. Stepping on a crack was impossible here, and so were the consequences, and the childish care to avoid them, and the wondering: Is it true? Must I beware? The kids wouldn't grow up as I had, I realized. But perhaps this was for the better.

In the neighborhood of my childhood, there were sidewalks and they were kept with care. Sometimes on Saturday mornings you'd see the old lady who lived on the corner, her head in a scarf and her feet in slippers, methodically sweeping every inch of the stretch outside her home. One summer new sidewalks were planned for the whole city. First, workmen came and broke up and hauled away the old slate walks. They'd been cracked and split by age, and they bore faint traces of chalk marks and the dim outlines of splattered bugs. Then the workmen laid down wood slats for borders and between them stretched wire mesh with squares so big you could put a fist into one. For weeks I watched diligently, early mornings when the milkman made his rounds, late nights when I should have been asleep, trying to catch the moment when they poured

1

the new concrete. But the summer dragged on, and nobody came to finish the job.

While I sat on the wood slats, balancing my Pro Keds on the wires, keeping a lookout for a city works truck, what I found instead was the music in the air. It had always been there in my neighborhood, that summer R&B, wafting from the transistor radios of passers-by, drifting over from a cookout in a nearby back yard, streaming from the cars parked at the curb outside the house of the Jamaican family across the street. But I'd never really heard it before, not until that summer. That summer I listened. I heard about gangster leans and puzzled over what sort of cool thing one might be. A woman sang almost in a moan about being someone's rocking chair, and I swayed along to the sound of her voice. And when the Undisputed Truth warned me about smiling faces, they did it on the back of an edgy groove that just about gave me goose bumps. I begged my mother until she bought me a little yellow radio, which I carried everywhere. I memorized the lyrics to just about every song that got enough airplay, and whenever one I knew came on, I lost myself in its familiar little world.

One night I stayed up so late with that radio pressed to my ear that I slept past breakfast the next day. My mother didn't wake me. Instead she waved me to the window when I came out to find her frying eggs and bacon in the kitchen. I gasped at what I saw and ran outside. Workmen had come through while I was sleeping and poured the concrete for the sidewalks. And it hadn't been too long ago, either, because the squares were still darkly damp at their centers. I looked at the apartment building, where my mother, who rose early, had been awake for hours. Why hadn't she gotten me up? How could she let me miss it? I slammed back inside, refused to eat breakfast, and parked myself sullenly in front of the television.

School started a few days later, and I began the fifth grade. Loaded down with my supplies—pens, pencils, erasers, binders, books, homework, and lunch—I left the radio home when I set out in the mornings. I felt uneasy walking along the continuous reel of dull gray ribbon under my feet. It should have been my guide and guardian, a sure way to where I had to go, but I had missed its creation and so it was too much a mystery to me. It might as well have fallen out of the sky.

Back then, during that summer, my mother kept a big clock-radio with an eight-track tape deck sitting on the table in the kitchen. It had an actual clock face, hands and all, next to the speaker on its front, and silver control knobs ran across the top of it where the handle was attached. She played it whenever she was in the kitchen cooking, and hummed along with whatever was playing, but she turned it off when we sat down to dinner. The three of us, my mother and I and Sean, my little brother, nearly filled up the tiny kitchen. We bumped plates and elbows all the time, and it didn't help that when Sean played with his food, my mother didn't seem to notice it and rarely told him to stop.

Our kitchen got pretty hot during the summer, and one evening in the most scorching part of July, I came up with a great idea. We could open the refrigerator and let the air inside it cool us off a little. Sean was making choo-choo noises, pushing a pile of string beans toward the edge of his plate. I tried out my idea on my mother, who looked up from under the huge Afro she wore, finished chewing, and said no.

"Why not?" I asked.

Sean whacked my glass of punch with his fork, and it chimed shrilly.

My mother smiled. She often did this when she was telling me no. She shook her head, and the big hoop earrings she wore stirred gently. "All the food would get spoiled, Miriam. You know that."

"We could turn it up colder," I said.

My mother laughed, just a little puff of air through her nose, and went back to eating.

"I don't see why not," I persisted.

"Coming in for a landing," Sean announced, and he popped a french fry into his mouth.

There was a shred of leaf in his hair, and a small twig. It was amazing the things he got in there that fell out when my mother brushed his head at night.

"Well?" I said.

Then Sean started rattling on about playing in the next-door neighbor kid's inflatable pool that afternoon. He named all the Scooby-Doo characters that he said were painted on the bottom of the pool, and my mother listened and nodded as he went on. While he spoke he arranged his french fries into a series of triangles on his plate, and when he ran out of space he started making tepees.

"Quit it, Sean," I told him. I was finished eating, but I stayed at the table.

"Quit what?" he said. One of his little structures fell and sent a couple of french fries onto the floor.

"See that?" I asked my mother.

She looked at me out of her large brown eyes for a moment, then she stood up and lifted away my plate and Sean's. "I think we're through for the night," she said as she took the plates to the sink.

When I looked over at Sean, he was sitting there quietly with his hands in his lap, waiting for her to come back. Sometimes it seemed like the air went out of him when she wasn't near. It got on my nerves, and not just because of him. Whatever it was, I felt it too.

My mother wasn't like most of the parents on the block, the ones who yelled a lot and stalked outside and grabbed a switch out of the hedges at the slightest provocation. This confused me. I wondered if her peculiar manner had something to do with the way she restored herself in the evenings, after she'd come home from work, fixed dinner, helped with homework, cleaned house, messed with bills and papers and envelopes on the coffee table while Flip Wilson or Andy Williams yammered on television, and put up her hair in braids that stood out like pipe cleaners. After she'd gotten Sean and me in bed, she tied her braids up in a scarf, went out on the front porch, and sat looking at the cars passing by in the street.

We lived in a big, brick corner building four stories high, four apartments to the floor. In the summer months the porch was a high-traffic area, with people coming and going until late into the evening, banging through the door, calling to friends driving down the block, getting a *whaa whaa* on the horn in reply. And of course there were the Jamaican men across the street, who rattled on loudly and burst out laughing from time to time. Sean's and my bedroom window opened onto the porch where my mother sat. She allowed us to leave the window open a few inches for air and, I suppose, so she could keep an ear out for trouble. She never stayed for long, only a minute or two some nights. It hardly seemed worth it to me for her to go to the trouble of dragging one of the kitchen chairs out there just for that. But she did.

Now and then, when there was a lull in the traffic of cars and bodies, I caught a snatch of her humming. I'd listen for the melody of a radio song, but she was humming something else, something with more relaxed rhythms and tunes that slid around in unpredictable ways. Was she thinking about my father, whom she never mentioned to us, who had left so long ago I didn't even remember him? I wished she would, but I doubted that she was. Somebody would fire a car engine and screech out into the street, tires pealing, drawing hoots and laughter from the Jamaican men. And on the other side of this racket, my mother continued uninterrupted, as if her humming came out of somewhere so deep no surface noise was going to disturb it.

Not that my mother was a quiet person. She drove us around in a lime-green Datsun hatchback that went off like a firecracker when she started it. The top of it was barely high enough to accommodate her Afro. The spools of silver bangle bracelets she wore on her wrists jangled against the steering wheel whenever she turned it sharply. Now and then she flicked the radio on and got a burst of static that reminded her it was broken, and she shut if off. And despite repeated trips to the repair shop, the car ran so loudly you could hear us coming a mile away.

She liked to take us out on Saturday mornings, when school and her job did not get in the way of our being together, she said. Sometimes she dragged us across town to visit Aunt Sophie, who was really Sean's and my great aunt and was too ensconced in her easy chair to keep us occupied for long. More often, though, she would drive right past all sorts of intriguing things in the city—stores and movie theaters, the library with its maze of dusty rooms

I wanted to explore—and carry us out into the countryside. The old turnpike was her favorite route. She would point out cows and horses and geese to Sean, who kept his face pressed to the window. Sometimes we stopped for ice cream.

One Saturday morning, during one of these trips, she looked over at me balled up in the passenger seat with my chin resting dully on my fist and my yellow transistor radio squeezed to my ear and said, "You're going to ruin the seats like that."

I uncurled myself and put my feet on the floor.

"You want to see something really boss?" she asked.

A dingy white barn with a leaning silo went by. "What?" I muttered.

"I'll take that as a yes," she said, and turned off the turnpike onto a gravel road. Branches slapped at the windows. Then the way opened up and a wide, flat expanse of land stretched out on either side of the road. In one field was a house, too far away to see well, and on the other side of the road was a clump of sad, low buildings that looked like they had been dumped there by someone who wanted to be rid of them. My mother pulled over. A big, chestnut-brown horse stood dazedly behind a white picket fence near us, but I wasn't interested in him and Sean had fallen asleep in the back.

"Wait just a minute," my mother said.

"Is he coming over here or something?" I asked, looking at the horse.

"Not as far as I know."

"I don't even have an apple." I knew the drill.

"Just wait a minute."

She was giving me a funny look, some kind of little secret smile, but I didn't know what the secret was so this only annoyed me. Why couldn't she just tell me things? She was supposed to be a mother, wasn't she, was supposed to know all kinds of stuff, not just about my father, either, but useful things, and how was I ever going to know what she really knew if she never told me? I started to curl up again, caught myself, and sat up straight. My mother reached over, rested her hand on the back of my neck, and rubbed her thumb up and down the crispy hair at my nape.

"You want to leave, Miri?" she asked.

I thought about it, but I couldn't make up my mind.

"You're getting big," my mother said, stroking me more slowly with her thumb. "School and work and all use up so much time. Every day you're different. It still surprises me."

A tractor or something droned in the distance.

"No, I'm not," I said.

"We all are," she said, "and that's the wonder, how it happens."

The droning was louder now, but when I looked out the windshield for a tractor I couldn't find one. My mother's finger fell still. I craned my neck, looking around.

"What is—"

And just like that it was upon us, an airplane so loud I thought it was about to crash into the car, but it got even louder and then I saw the broad wings and the underside with its landing gear and the roar exploded in my head. The car trembled in the grip of a force far beyond anything its little engine could muster, and I was shaken out of my boredom, out of all thoughts of the city. The plane passed over us, flying low, and skidded down onto what must have been a runway that I couldn't see from where we'd parked.

My mother said something. I unclapped my arms from my head. I had scooted all the way across the seat and was pressed up under her arm, where she must have felt my heart hammering. The plane slowed and turned, then rolled toward the tumble of buildings, a rural airport.

"You've been buzzed, Miri," she said in my ear.

Sean was awake now, chattering away in the back seat, and she turned around and answered his questions. Then I started laughing, and she said, "So what's so funny, huh?" but the way she said it, I knew that she knew.

"That *was* boss," I finally managed.

My mother pulled back onto the road and drove on. We stayed off the main highway, rolling through fields dotted with muddy cowponds and marked by trees planted in lines as neat as hedges. "C'mon, Miri, drive for a while," my mother said. "Just the steering wheel." I thought she was kidding and just giggled, but she took one hand off the wheel and rested it on the seat behind my shoulders. I slid closer to her. The road was flat and straight and led into a stand of trees far ahead. It would have taken little coordination. Sean, who was quiet now in the back seat, could have done it. I looked at my mother's profile, her eyes fixed ahead on the road, and knew she was taking me in without even looking at me. The way she did, I now realized, in the kitchen when she didn't seem to be watching Sean or me. And this made me suddenly uneasy, that she had been observing me and was doing so now in some kind of odd way that I could not even see. The next thing I knew, we had plunged into the trees and the road looped and turned, and my mother took her hand off the seat to drive.

I waited for her to say something. I thought for sure she would give me another chance. But the moment had passed, and all she asked me, a little later, was whether I wanted to stop by Dairy Queen.

It took twenty minutes or so for us to get back to the city, and when we finally got close to home, my mother tried to blow the horn at a car double-parked in the middle of the street, and nothing happened. It was broken. Sean noticed right away and, as we drove around the parked car, wailed in the shrillest imitation of a car horn a human being could possibly have made. A man in the driver's seat of the car gave us a puzzled look as we passed by. Then, at the corner, when a big, old station wagon took its time moving through the intersection after the light turned green, Sean howled like a demon again.

I turned around and glared at him.

"I wanna be the horn!" he blurted.

"You wanna be Mommy's horn?" my mother asked. "Just wait till I tell you, okay?"

"Okay."

Then she threw on the brakes abruptly because a line of cars was stopped in front of us. People up ahead were honking at the delay. Two-story houses with weather-beaten clapboards and sunbleached paint lined the block, and outside of them, in the warm summer air, people trimmed hedges, stood chatting, or pushed baby strollers. A few watched the traffic from porch seats.

"What is it now?" my mother sighed.

Taking this as a cue, Sean began: "Meeeeeeeeeeeep." My mother laughed at him, and he did it again. "Meeeeeeeeeeeeeeep."

I wanted to throttle him, and I might even have turned around and done it if my mother had not left me speechless by saying, "Toooooooooooooooooooot. That's a train horn."

Sean, of course, screeched his own version at twice the volume. Then the two of them fell into a fit of giggling.

Traffic was at a dead halt. Some people in the street were staring at us now. And then a man popped his head into the driver's-side window and looked at us.

"Something wrong?" he asked.

"Oh, no," my mother laughed, "not a thing. We're just having fun while we wait."

The man took this in and mulled it over for a minute. He was older than my mother, gray at his temples, dressed in a neat plaid shirt and wearing rimless glasses that sharpened his black eyes. He didn't smile. I caught his eye when he shifted his gaze for a moment, but he looked back at my mother almost immediately, and just like that, I hated him. I knew he would act as if he'd found a perfectly normal family inside our car.

"Some fool stalled up there," he said. "They pushing it out of the way. Just be a minute."

"Thank you," my mother smiled.

Then he was gone, ambling off in a hitching gait, never looking back. And a moment later, I was gone, too. I jumped out of the car, slammed the door behind me, and began trudging home by myself because I wasn't about to stay in that lunatic asylum of a car with them. My mother called me a few times, but in her usual voice, not like my friends' parents, who bellowed down the block in a way you didn't dare ignore. So I paid no attention and kept going. Home wasn't far, anyway. But the sidewalks were still ripped up here, the concrete yet to come, so there was nowhere to walk, really. I balanced along the wood slats for a while, then picked my way along the churned up dirt between them and the curb until I tripped and fell on my knees. I wasn't hurt, but I was filthy. I didn't care. I walked the rest of the way in the street, daring cars to swipe me.

Not much later, one day after dinner, I went outside and sat on a slat and looked up and down the ditch that was still not a sidewalk. There was still no sign of the trucks, the concrete mixers I had seen in other parts of the city, their vaults turning slowly on their beds as they drove down the street. How long were they going to take? It seemed like forever already. Then it occurred to me that I could go find them instead of just waiting. They had to be working somewhere in the city, and maybe it wasn't far away.

I didn't have a bike, but my neighbor Derrick did, so I borrowed his sky-blue ten-speed. It was too big for me, though, and I didn't get twenty feet before I pitched myself over the handlebars and cut a gash over my eye. My mother nearly swallowed her tongue when she got a look at the blood from what was really only a small cut, and when she got me cleaned up and had applied a Band-Aid, she told me to stay inside for the rest of the evening in case I had a concussion. "I mean it, Miriam," she said, testing my scalp for lumps with the tips of her fingers. I waited about half an hour, until she was in the kitchen washing dishes, and then slipped back outside.

"You look all weird," Derrick said when I found him in his back yard, popping caps against the walk with a piece of a brick. He was a dark, long-headed boy, slow in speech, clad all the time in a dress shirt and polished leather shoes.

"It's just a Band-Aid," I snapped. Pictures were tumbling through my mind, images of my mother, wiping her hands on her dish towel, discovering me gone. I wanted to set things in motion, wanted to find her limits. "Where's Ruthie's bike?" I asked impatiently.

Ruthie was Derrick's younger sister, and letting me borrow her bike was something Derrick was reluctant to do. But I convinced him it'd be okay if he went along with me, and we set off, Derrick riding his ten-speed, me on Ruthie's purple banana-seat bike with rainbow straws on all the wheel spokes.

We passed through familiar streets, then ventured farther and farther, past stores and businesses we knew only from seeing them go by from a car window. Of course we had to stop and investigate the Diebold Tool and Dye Company and peek in through the open back door of Half Moon Lanes, where the sound of crashing balls and pins echoed to a deafening volume. Mitzi's High Life delayed us until Derrick figured out that the place was a bar. We kept making our way back to the sidewalk bed and pushing a little farther, until finally we found twilight falling around us and Ruthie's bike unfit for travel. The back tire had a flat. We couldn't have been more than a twenty-minute ride from home, but it seemed like a daylong journey by foot.

"My mama's going to kill me," Derrick moaned.

I told him to go on, and he pedaled off with great relief.

Left alone now, I followed the ripped-up walkway home, pushing Ruthie's bike along in the street. The neighborhood I found myself in was less busy than ours, the houses set farther back from the street, some of them enclosed by low chain-link fences. Nobody was hanging around in the cars neatly parked at the curb, and no music drifted on the air. There were lights in the windows, but only on the lower floors, and now and then silhouettes moved silently back and forth behind the drapes. I don't know how long I spent walking through there, but I must have lingered for a while, lulled by the peacefulness of the place. When I finally reached my own block, all the light had drained from the sky and it was night.

Something was happening. Even from the far end of the block I sensed the knot of commotion. The hovering red glows of tail-lights showed that there were several cars stopped in the street. When I got closer, I could hear shouting and see people standing out on their porches to get a look at whatever was going on. Then I was in a crowd of people pressed in among the parked cars and signposts and trees and trash cans, speaking in hushed voices or not at all. I found a girl who lived upstairs from me, and she told me it was Abbie Rule from down the street, struck by a car. Out where the crowd thinned, I caught a glimpse of a bicycle wheel bent around like a pretzel. In the distance, a siren wailed its approach. My mother, the girl told me before moving away for a better view, had been out here a few minutes ago looking for me.

I kept waiting for Abbie to emerge from the crowd, brushing herself off, waving away concern; but she didn't. The ambulance came and went without my ever seeing her. Not until the next morning would she come home with her arm in the cast she would wear the rest of the summer. One of the Jamaican men lifted the twisted bicycle out of the street in one hand and carried it away, out of sight, and only then did the crowd begin to disperse. They went slowly, peeling away from the outer circle to the inner, until finally everyone had gone and nothing but the empty street remained under the blue-white glow of the street lamps.

I parked Ruthie's bike behind Derrick's house, near the cellar doors, and went home. The crowd and the mangled wheel and the ambulance were all whirling around in my head, but as soon as I pushed open our front door the seriousness of my own situation hit me. In the dark apartment, light came from the kitchen but there was no sound, and I could not figure out where my mother was. I looked around, straining to hear. Finally I could stand the suspense no longer, and I reached behind me, where the door stood slightly ajar, and slammed it shut. My mother rushed out of the kitchen, her eyes too full of light, still, to make me out by the door. Then she saw me, and came to me and caught me up in her arms. When she grabbed me, the only sense I could make of her was a great pressure of flesh and bone pressing into my body. Then she was my mother, squeezing the wind out of me and moaning, "Oh my God, Miriam, oh my God," over and over until she fell to trembling and dampening my cheeks with her tears.

I froze in her arms. All of this for Abbie Rule? My mother hardly knew her. I hardly knew Abbie myself. She was my age, but she'd just moved into the neighborhood a few weeks earlier. Of course I hoped that Abbie would be okay, but my mother's reaction astonished me. All this for Abbie Rule, it was too much, too much, and when my mother quieted down and her grip finally loosened, I was so embarrassed that I ran off to Sean's and my bedroom and shut the door.

I don't know how long I stayed like that, sitting on my bed with my knees drawn up to my chin. Sean was asleep, snoring faintly, a stuffed dog clutched to his side. If my mother went out on the porch that night, with her chair and her humming, I never heard her. I think I must have missed her entirely.

Tonight, with the kids in bed and Robert reading in the bedroom, I slip downstairs to the family room, disconnect the CD deck, and plug in the turntable. I put on one of the old 45's I've brought down from a carton I keep in the back of a closet, and the record is so old, so hardened by time, I wonder whether the needle can coax a sound from it. I sit back as the needle *chuff chuff chuffs* toward the song.

For a while, around the time I began to think of myself as an adult, I dismissed all the summer R&B music I had loved as a trunkful of clichés. Then, when I passed thirty, I figured my lingering attachment to it was nothing but a harmless weakness for sentimental claptrap. I congratulated myself on being so astute and granted myself the indulgence of the occasional loud, off-key rendition of "Show and Tell" or "Band of Gold" in the bathroom shower. Now I slip away often to spin my dusty 45's over and over, because those old songs, carved in vinyl, give me a kind of release I can find nowhere else in this house.

This evening hasn't been a good one. The rift between Robert and me has probably grown past the point where we could repair it. We often do what we are doing tonight, dwell in separate parts of our common home. The flat sensation of repetition hangs over our marriage like a shadow, and we speak to one another in used-up words. I believe he is seeing another woman. The children aren't enough to patch things over, though we've relied on them for years to do it. Probably since the time Simone was five or six and started having trouble in school, and we went through phonics and tutors and psychologists and everything else we could lay hands on to defeat a problem that required only a pair of glasses.

The muted horns on the record subside, and the Chairmen of the Board ease into the last verse of "Give Me Just a Little More Time."

And the rift grows worse for the silliest of reasons: because Robert thinks that I don't notice it. Because he thinks that it doesn't really bother me. He thinks he alone is affected. Why don't you ever close your eyes when you're daydreaming, he wants to know. Why? And when my wallet was stolen and the police returned it intact, minus only the money and credit cards: why don't you have snapshots of Simone and Bobbie and me in those little plastic sleeves? Eh? And why don't you ever tell me about your childhood?

He tells me about his. Big family. Grands and great grands.

Cousins galore. Not much money, rattletrap used cars that nearly flew apart on the highway, hand-me-down jeans, sneakers, toys, hand-me-down coloring books with the pictures already filled in. Sleepovers, fights with the neighbor kids, the time he and his brothers almost burned the house down. The whole brood gets together down in Winston-Salem for a big reunion every few years.

I've told him that my father left us not long after my brother was born and my mother raised us alone. Robert fidgets, hangs his lovely, soft head full of black whorls, laces his graceful caramel fingers across his knees and waits patiently for more. He's a patient man. He's been waiting for years to hear the rest that he knows I must be holding back.

Maybe he's right, that there's something more.

The song fades out, and the needle returns to its cradle.

Should I tell Robert about that night? My mother holding me, the flood of her grief for Abbie Rule threatening to sweep me under? Even now I think back to the way I broke her rules that night, my rude departure, the duration of my disappearance, the lateness of the hour when I came dragging in like some drunken sot of a husband, too thoughtless and lazy to bother bringing an excuse. And I get stuck on what is missing, what I keep groping back in time to search for but never find: her rage, her fury. The anger that might have melted me.

Mud Show

September, 1884. Here and there a tree displayed a smattering of yellow and gold where leaves had turned prematurely in advance of the approaching New England fall. But these shone dully, for most of the sunlight from above vanished into the thick canopy of oaks and hickories that meshed their branches above the road. Distracted by the beauty, nudged along perhaps by the gloom, a caravan of people and animals moved—who knows how quickly—through the northern Connecticut woods. They traveled along an old dirt road that meandered through low hills past the jagged rims of caved-in wells and half-buried foundation walls. Along such roads, there is always the mute company of a stone fence which follows you like the last, lingering thoughts of the first child who died up there when the settlement was new and hopeful. *God protect Mother and Father. I killed the lamb, I never meant it, I'm sorry, I'm sorry. Lord have mercy on my soul.*

They were headed for Saybury, some miles distant yet when the whole line drew to a sudden halt. The air had been stuffy with sound for some time, plagued by low, distant rumblings that most of them took for the sound of blasting despite the frequency with which it came. Perhaps, they thought, a road was being cleared with dynamite. The progress of roads and bridges, the advance of science and industry across the land, was cherished by the rest of society no more strongly than among the performers, animal handlers, and trinket vendors who paused, now, with their ears to the wind. To believe was to belong, and they believed fiercely in the modern world. They knew nothing of Whitman but in lighter moods might have imagined themselves distant cousins, kin in time if not by fortune, to his throngs pulsing along the decks of the Brooklyn Ferry, their eyes turned ahead to Manhattan. But what these people felt as they stood among their stinking animals and overloaded carts, among leaves drifting down from trees stretching as far as the eye could see, was altogether different.

At the head of the line a tall, lanky man named Cheffal climbed onto a rock outcropping to hear above the murmur of the circus train. His whey-colored cheeks were shaven smooth, and around his head blew straight, coarse, black hair befitting a horse's tail. His narrow eyes were weak, but his ears were sharp, and everyone listened for him to speak. He scrambled down from the rock before he did, and then he turned to the two or three men nearest him. "Thunder," he told them simply, and walked on.

As his words were repeated down the line, the booming came again in a rolling cascade of explosions that silenced them all. But Cheffal waved his arm in a long, arcing motion like whipping, and the entire troupe gathered itself to follow him. If this was what thunder sounded like in Connecticut, they wished to finish their performances and move south again, out of these choking woods, as soon as they could.

Cheffal had been hired to manage H. C. Hutherford's American Floating Circus three months before. Given the rumors attached to his name at the time, he had been lucky to find employment at all, and he told himself this often. He told himself so now as a light rain, trapped high above by the canopy of trees, began to fall. The knowledge should have eased the cramping hold on his mind of all his problems—the dwindling supply of animal feed, the loss of one of the snake handler's two pythons, which had been run over by a wagon, the defection of his two "Inca sisters" back home to Kerhonksen, New York, and the odd behavior of his elephant trainer, Bettoc, who insisted on rest stops, dirt baths, and impromptu dirgelike serenades from the weary band for his lone charge, Zulu, every mile of their journey.

Cheffal told himself he was lucky, but he believed himself cursed. The failures that had forced him to join Hutherford had not been his fault, not the fire on the mushroom farm, not the poisonings from his Lumbar Formula, none of it. These had been acts of God for which he bore no blame, and he seethed at the fact that they had led him here, to a floating circus which no longer floated. A year ago the barge that used to house the circus had sunken off the coast of Long Island, and down with it went the seaside resort shows, most of the profits, and all of the menagerie except for a monkey and the snakes.

Still Hutherford had insisted on reorganizing, adding Bettoc and his elephant, and going on, and Cheffal had had no other option but to become his instrument. He had sent no proceeds back to Hutherford in months, yet he had not heard a word of complaint. They had spent the summer tramping through Pennsylvania, then lower New York (avoiding the city itself, the territory of the larger circuses allied against the invasion of mud shows like Hutherford's), and finally Connecticut, where people seemed under some warping influence that flattened their tongues in speech and chiseled their manners into a chary nastiness admitting no joy or generosity. They'd entered more than one town where not a single tavern owner or storekeeper had allowed the posting of handbills on his walls in return for free tickets to the show. A farmer had shot at them during the night for pausing at the edge of his field. When they paraded through the green at Litchfield, children balked at their wheezing accordion and threw rocks at them, screaming for a real calliope.

The rain came through, wetting Cheffal's hair. Two more weeks, perhaps less, and they would head south for the winter season. He kicked at stones as he walked. Connecticut had the stoniest ground, be it field or road, he had ever seen. A thousand stones for every person, if not a million, stone fences, stone houses, and it would not surprise him if families sat down to a stew made of stones for their dinner. Still he walked, as was his wont, when he could have ridden a horse or wagon like most of the rest of them. And as he walked he looked ahead at the mule of the nigger guide they had hired when Hutherford's agent, Spitz, had disappeared in Torrington. There had probably been foul play; no money had vanished with Spitz, not even his own. But Cheffal had grown tired of the fat

17

way Spitz filled his suits, the ever-wet mouth, and the voice as soft as a woman's, and he had not been sorry enough about his disappearance to delay the circus and waste a chance for income.

The guide turned around just then and looked at him as if he'd read Cheffal's mind, and Cheffal gave him a look to tell him, eyes ahead. He was about to say something to him when Bettoc, who had trotted up beside him, tapped him on the shoulder.

Bettoc gasped, trying to catch his breath. That damned Cheffal kept up a pace that taxed the horses and set the wagons to straining their axles almost to the point of splitting or losing a wheel, and yet he kept on. He had spoken to George Mattie, their guide, and tried to convince him to slow the procession down, but Mattie answered to Cheffal of course and knew where his pay was coming from, and nobody could blame the man for ignoring his request. Sweat beaded on his hatless brow as he tugged at Cheffal's shoulder.

"Mr. Cheffal," he huffed. "Mr. Cheffal, sir, Zulu must be watered."

Cheffal threw him a sidelong glance, as if surprised, and Bettoc marveled once again at his density: that even a criminal, even so practical a man, could not understand the simple need of an animal to drink. All of it gave him a sense of foreboding that he was helpless to do anything about, out here in the middle of nowhere, far from the little family circus he had signed on with when he first arrived in this country. But that circus had failed, as he feared this one would also. With a man like Cheffal leading them, though, that was hardly the worst of his fears.

He watched as Cheffal looked behind him at Zulu, then forward at Mattie. Cheffal raised a hand and shouted at the procession to halt, and others echoed the call back down the line. Then he nodded to Mattie, who brought his mule around, climbed down, and slowly scanned the woods around him for the best route to the nearest stream.

George Mattie. If you can stand the dust, the cobwebs, and the mold, find his likeness in charcoal on a forgotten page in a forgotten book in the stacks of a neglected library or two, or three perhaps, that have not yet discarded the volume. The caption: Black

George, hunting guide. And, since he was no colorful circus handler or eccentric financier, that is all you will be told. His straw hat apparently jaunty, his brow carved in woodland sagacity, he seems the shadow counterpart of the celebrated, rustic Adirondack guide, beloved of the Victorian-era new-money classes who rode into the wilderness by train, seeking the sublime. But George Mattie never lived and breathed in the Adirondacks.

He climbed down from Fannie and walked back through those thick Connecticut woods to where Cheffal and Bettoc waited, the one of them still and impatient, the other weaving a little where he stood. Neither of them struck him singly as a remarkable white man. Men like Cheffal preferred their own company above that of any other person or thing, but spent their lives corralling and chasing the people and things of men who could pay for the service. Bettoc would have left no impression at all had he not tried to be unimpressive. During the long stretches of travel, when he simply walked alongside his elephant, patting its shoulder, speaking gently into its enormous flap of ear, it was as if he were absorbed into it. But he stopped the train often, and each time became more apologetic for it, until after a while even George Mattie was surprised to feel an urge to cut him with a switch, a measure he never even thought to take with Fannie.

"Look," said Cheffal as George approached, "we can't keep stopping for that thing. We got to get there tonight and it's almost dark now."

"Get where?" Bettoc answered. "Where is it so important to get that you want to kill us all just to get there? Where?"

"What is it, now, Cranberry or something?" Cheffal asked George.

"Saybury," George said.

"And how far?"

"About five miles."

He looked at Bettoc. "You want to sleep at all tonight, you keep moving after this."

Behind them, a few of the ropewalkers had dismounted from one of the wagons and were stretching their legs. George could tell who they were because they were small, as he was, and their feet turned out, both the two men's and the woman's, as if in disgust at the ground that they picked their way across.

"You got ten minutes!" Cheffal yelled at them.

At this, others began emerging from the wagons, their clothes, even out in the woods, screaming shades of red and purple and orange, some of them in feathered hats, a few men bare to the waist. A monkey began screeching. George watched as they fanned out into the woods, tall and short, thin and fat, the bent and the straight, some of them with arms locked as they went, nobody speaking a word, and wondered, as he had done watching them depart before, why any of them would ever come back to this. Bettoc had asked him the day he had joined them in order to lead them to Saybury whether George would like to play a cannibal in the show. The others would do him up in bones and feathers and paint, he could growl and spit at white people, he could scream and howl at them all and they would laugh, thinking him amusing, never knowing a thing. Bettoc had grinned conspiratorially the whole time he spoke, as if he expected George to jump at the chance. He had told Bettoc that he did not care to join his profession. When Bettoc's face fell, he realized that Bettoc had not understood, until then, what kind of profession he belonged to.

"And you got five," Cheffal said to George. "Get moving."

He found a stream not far away, one through woods so abnormally thin that Bettoc followed him, leading Zulu along, and the elephant simply snapped away the small saplings in his path. There was far less noise as the beast moved than George would have imagined, and yet he felt as if something was bearing down on him, a feeling which raised the hairs on the back of his neck. At the stream he got out of the way, and Bettoc led the animal in and left it to suck up water in its trunk and empty it again and again into its mouth.

Bettoc came over to where he squatted against a tree. Why couldn't he just stay with his animal, George wondered as the man approached. Bettoc tried to squat also, but when his pinstripe trousers tightened over his legs he stood up again and, in the middle of the woods, whispered.

"Is there a way we could get him to stop for a few hours?" he asked.

This was the last thing George wanted. Another five miles, a few predawn hours at the edge of Saybury, a day for the circus there, and he would be paid and set free of them all. He could go home to his cabin, his traps, the peace of no company but Fannie for miles. But Bettoc was leaning toward him as if they shared a secret desire.

"Is there a way, do you know? Some way?" Bettoc's blue eyes looked almost delirious under the damp spikes of his brown hair. "He is sick."

"Sick?" George asked. "The elephant?"

It was looking over at them, flapping its ears slowly.

"Yes, yes!" Bettoc exclaimed. Then, whispering again, "It's a thing with the glands, you know, that comes on them sometimes, and they cannot help themselves—"

A cracking sound signaled the approach of Cheffal's messenger, a laconic boy of twelve or thirteen by the name of Garrick.

"He say come on," Garrick said.

He stood there looking at them, and Bettoc sighed and went back to his elephant. He stood at the edge of the water, staring out over it, while the beast lay its trunk over his shoulder. Watching them, Garrick plucked a piece of grass, put it between his teeth, and laughed at Bettoc.

"Day it piss on him," he said to George, "he surely gonna drown."

After a while the rain, which had never become heavy, ceased, and a thin, wavering alto voice rose up from the caravan in song. But none of the others took it up, and after a few bars it stopped. It reminded George of his days on the canal, the way he would pass another boat sometimes, and there would be a whole family, father, children, sometimes even a mother with a baby above deck, singing in a language he could not understand. And at those times he thought of his own wife, made her up in his mind, of course, for he had no real wife and no family besides an aunt in Albany. Thought of her just back from the woods, her skirts full of blackberries, her strong hands wrapped around the load, her soft hair pulled up and away from the face she turned aside shyly. Her feet bare. But it wasn't shyness that turned her face away, as she came up a path and the sun-drunk yellow jackets hovered around her. It was that he could not see what he did not believe.

Ahead loomed a fork in the road where the left, he knew, led to high land and the right down to a place where the caravan could cross through shallows only a few inches deep into the next county. He turned Fannie to the right and led the circus downhill. The stone fence disappeared and in its place a thick bed of ferns spread from the road back into the trees on either side of them. The group, even Cheffal, was slowing behind him even though George stopped periodically to wait rather than fall in with their pace. When George worked like this, as an occasional guide, leading hunters up from New York, usually, or surveyors mapping lands for a resort, this often happened. Their shoes were city shoes, their legs attuned to the terrain of settled places. They accused him sometimes of leading them the hard way on purpose and swore at him or cheated him of the pay they had agreed to in retaliation. And when rid of them later, as he roasted a fish or rabbit over his fire while Fannie ate from her feed bag behind him, he mused at how they failed to see that they themselves were doing to him what they accused him of doing to them. But this irony was a brief amusement he shared only with himself, and it burned up quickly in his fire.

He paused again, turned Fannie halfway to face the caravan, and waited. For these people, this kind of travel was nothing new. They were road people who understood necessity and, he would have thought, would not waste time whining in the face of it. Perhaps it was the influence of Cheffal at the head of the line. Perhaps that of Bettoc at the end of it. He himself was glad to not have to ride between them.

As he sat waiting on Fannie, the elephant trumpeted and reared up into the air. From where George watched it looked different in motion, heavier, huger yet than the boulder it had seemed like earlier. Someone screamed, and the startled team of horses nearest the elephant dragged a wagon half off the road before their driver could halt them. Cheffal wheeled around and ran to the end of the line. The elephant came down, whipped its trunk about, and backed several steps up the road, weaving from side to side as it went.

Mud Show

George dismounted and went to the errant wagon, a broad, tall one with its parti-colored paint chipping steadily away. Several women had already alighted, and the man who had been driving stood looking at the front wheels mired in mud from the rain. He wore an old broadcloth shirt and a wide-brimmed hat with a piece missing in the back.

"Danged elephant," he hissed.

And when a murmur of assent went up behind him, George turned and saw he was surrounded by them, the same ones he had seen drifting out into the woods in their colored tunics and pants. One old man held the monkey like a child. Another wore long graying hair and a beard of the same color that hung down past his knees. There were the aerialists, even tinier up close, all of them in white, and behind them several men who might have been found shooting dice in an alley outside a tavern in any nearby town. A few of them looked at him, and George quickly turned away, but almost immediately he felt a hand on his arm.

He shook it off and moved sideways, quickly, deeper into the crowd. They were chattering now, most of them unintelligibly, some in voices distorted into fluting or rasping sounds. George reached the edge of the crowd and looked at Fannie and thought to himself, perhaps he had best simply go, leave these people to themselves. It would mean a lot of money lost, a week's work gone for nothing, but that had happened before and he had managed to get by until something else, fruit-picking or odd jobs, came along. Fannie, yards away from him, lifted her head and looked down the road. He moved around the corner of the wagon into the woods.

Just then a group of men pulling at the wagon shifted it, and the monkey screamed and jumped from the handler's arms. It ran right past George into the woods. The old man ran after it, followed by two others, and their shirts bobbed for a few moments before disappearing into the trees.

"All right!" shouted Cheffal. He had come up behind the crowd and now climbed onto the side of the mired wagon. "Get back to the wagons! Now! Back to the wagons!"

They stopped talking and looked at him and stood there.

"You heard me!" Cheffal screamed.

None of them moved. George looked toward the end of the caravan, where he could see Bettoc trying to coax along the elephant, which had turned back up the road. He glanced again at Fannie. He would wait until they all moved, he decided, and then he would make his way back to Fannie. But they did not move.

"We ain't been paid in months!" yelled a woman's voice.

Cheffal glowered at her. "And you won't be, Emelda, for back talk!"

She didn't reply. Some of them stirred then, and the rest followed them toward the horses and wagons. The colored tunics began to disappear as they climbed back inside the wagons, and as they went George slipped away and hoisted himself up onto Fannie.

But Cheffal looked his way and beckoned to him, and George, sure that crossing the man just now would not be wise, turned Fannie and rode her back toward the line. As he did, he decided that Cheffal alone among them would not have questioned the hardness of the route that he had chosen for Hutherford's circus. No, Cheffal would have expected it.

He heard it from a half mile away and still he rode on because it gave him time to think. But the water grew louder as the road dipped down and soon there was no doubt as to the situation. One last bend, and George drew Fannie up and faced the river, now muddied and swollen well beyond its normal banks, from which the swirling water had plucked loose the weeds and branches that spun in its currents.

Cheffal, now on horseback, rode up beside him a minute later.

"How do we get over it?" he asked. "Where's the bridge?"

"No bridge," George said. "It's usually shallows here. Rain," and he looked up at the dimming sky, "rain must of fell heavy up north."

"That little bit of rain?"

"Wasn't little back up in the hills."

"So what do we do?"

"Go back."

George watched Cheffal digest this idea and decided to explain as little about the route as possible. They would have to double back several miles and follow a winding road through hillier lands, and their arrival at Saybury would probably be delayed by a day. Cheffal said nothing, just rode to the first wagon and began to lead it in a wide, slow circle that turned it back along the road. George looked once more at the water, which was too strong for Fannie on her old legs to cross, and turned around.

When most of the wagons were moving again, George rode up past the few still pointed at the river and then to Bettoc, who was stroking his elephant and talking quietly to it. He stopped and waited until Bettoc noticed him, but Bettoc regarded him with unfocused eyes. George looked at the elephant, which he had grown accustomed to without ever really seeing clearly, and its stench repelled him. When he gazed up at its huge bulk, he pulled Fannie back a step without meaning to. The black-gray skin seemed pitted and lined by a century's wear, and a wet stain darkened the old, creviced face. The tusks that sprang from its head could not have been meant for anything but killing, he was sure, and yet its face was all calmness. Into its black eye, it seemed, had gone all of Bettoc's self-possession, and there it would stay, preserved, until Bettoc was able to reclaim it. That eye regarded George now, waiting. Waiting.

He pushed Fannie to a trot then, and went forward along the line without looking back at them.

At the fork in the road where he had directed the line downhill to the river, George was far enough ahead of them to stop and wait, and yet he continued on the way the caravan had come. He could feel a pull in Fannie's stride, but he pushed her around a bend, out of sight of the fork, before he allowed her to slow down. It was probably her right, rear hoof, which bothered her now and again. There seemed to be some flaw, invisible to the eye, in that hoof.

He stopped then and waited. It occurred to him, and not for the first time, that were he to be struck dead right now, not one soul would miss him. When he was a boy, being raised by his aunt in Albany, he would speak her name three, four, even five times before she looked up from her washboard or the ball of dough she

25

was furiously kneading; and even then, her eyes would say . . . oh. And the men in the orchards, weary and brotherly after a day of picking apples, invited him to share a bottle by calling him Black George, same as the whites did. Cheffal and his circus would forget who had quietly, uncomplainingly, led their miserable band from Torrington all the way to Saybury. If this were not entirely true of Bettoc, it mattered little; George would be doing his best to forget him and his damned elephant, too, as soon as possible.

He wiped his forehead. He was sweating. Normally he felt best at moments like this, alone among the trees and the cawing of crows and the slight haze of water in the air. He could easily ride on now, while he was far ahead of them all, lose himself in the enveloping solitude of the woods he knew so well and let Cheffal and the rest of them find their way on their own. It was what he'd wanted to do for days. But he didn't move. He was still sitting there, hot and rigid, when Garrick's bony figure came loping around the bend and hailed him with the wave of an arm.

"Hey!" the boy yelled as he trotted up. "He say, why we ain't take that other road?"

George looked at him.

"You hear me talking to you? What you got to say?"

George leaned forward until his cheek was near Fannie's ear. His strange disquiet nudged him on.

"You run off with the circus, didn't you?" he asked, his voice hard and annoyed.

Now Garrick, hands in pockets, shoulders slouched, stared at him.

"You was eight or nine, right? And it looked like heaven, all them colors, all them animals and people from all over the place? But it ain't no heaven, is it. *Is it?*"

Garrick looked, suddenly, like a different boy, one stripped clean of the insouciance that had seemed to infect him to his core. He backed away a few steps, stumbled over a rock and caught himself. His mouth twisted.

"I'm going back," he said flatly. "You tell him yourself."

And to George's surprise, he turned and ran down the road.

Fannie sidled a step or two downhill before George halted her.

He stared at the spot where Garrick had rounded the bend and disappeared from sight, and as he did he stopped wondering what had drawn the boy into Cheffal's raggedy band. Now he wondered what Garrick must have been trying to leave behind. That was part of it too, the part, most likely, that made sense of the rest. All the times he'd seen the boy, running back and forth with Cheffal's messages, shining Cheffal's boots, hovering about like a lackey, and George had, until now, never thought of this. Not once.

Fannie gave a low, tired mutter. George leaned forward and stroked the large, dark flowers that were her ears. It was something he'd never known an animal to like, except for Fannie. From her nostrils there came, almost inaudible, a little snort of pleasure.

Not long afterward, Cheffal appeared, alone, riding a big chestnut mare, a cap on his head. George waited for him. Cheffal stopped when his horse nosed Fannie.

"Well?" he asked, nodding over his shoulder at the fork George had bypassed.

"They got a bridge there," George said. "It'll take the horses and wagons, but not the elephant."

Cheffal looked at him a moment, then he smiled, then he slapped his own leg, laughing. "Boy," he said, "you got one hell of a nerve, leading us all over creation when there's a bridge right here." He turned his horse back, adding, "I'll decide what it'll hold. Ain't much left of this damned circus anyway." He spat on the ground and suddenly became serious. "Won't be long before I'm free of it, too."

With that he rode off and left George sitting there. George was, he realized, free to go. Cheffal was letting him leave. It was clear that before he'd even finished talking, he'd dismissed George entirely.

George looked down the road at the shifting ferns, the trunks of trees and the shapes of leaves losing their clarity in the fading light. Then he turned Fannie and coaxed her, at a slow trot that would not overtax the bad hoof, back downhill.

When he caught up with them, they were already crossing the bridge over the gorge. Sandstone cliffs fell down from the green highlands to the water below, which roared over and around boulders. Cheffal was leading the train across. One after another, teams of horses stepped up onto the bridge, and the wagons rattled up onto the span behind them. It was a cement bridge with iron arches undergirding it, and in the gathering twilight, the entire structure blurred more and more into the planes and crevices of the far cliff, until the wagons appeared to be moving without support. Their rocking and swaying eased, their bodies glided smoothly. Painted lions and tigers, a pair of golden mermaids, red, blue, and yellow swirls and curlicues, all came clear and flowed along in a moment of transitory grace, until quickly, very quickly, the last wagon reached the far side and staggered onto the dirt as Cheffal waved it on.

Had George Mattie known what would happen next, perhaps he would not have gone back down the road to H. C. Hutherford's circus. If he had been clairvoyant, had conjured, in his mind's eye, pictures of the newsprint bearing the wild stories to which witnesses would swear, without blushing, at a Negro's trial—at his trial—perhaps. Instead, he watched as the men who did Cheffal's bidding surrounded the elephant, dragged Bettoc away from it, and began to drive it toward the bridge. It moved in tiny, mincing steps, backing up gingerly as it swung its trunk and tusks at the small, howling mob. At one point it caught a man who got too close on one of its tusks and flung him into the roadside brush. A moment of astonished silence fell over the men. Then their comrade rose and shook himself, clearly intact, and they began their work again.

Bettoc was on his knees at the roadside, spitting blood and teeth, where Cheffal's men had thrown him. His trousers torn, he was crawling slowly toward the commotion in front of the bridge when George reached him. At first George could neither get his attention nor arrest his slow, plodding progress toward his elephant. His mind seemed gone to memory, or at least to where such things as he found himself facing now did not happen.

Only when George blocked his way with Fannie did Bettoc look at him. Beyond words, beyond speech, he merely drooled a string of saliva and blood.

George pushed Bettoc up onto Fannie's back. A heavy man, deadweight as flour, he let himself crumple and be spread like a loaded sack across Fannie. George whispered in Fannie's ear, coaxing her. At first she balked at the excess weight, but then she consented and took a lurching step, then two, then three down the road. The elephant, seeing Bettoc, ceased backing up. It began, instead, to slash its way away from the bridge, toward him.

With one hand George led Fannie, with the other he steadied Bettoc. They moved slowly. Still, the elephant, fixated on Bettoc, pushed back its knot of tormentors and advanced another step. George glanced up the road where the elephant would soon come crashing along after Bettoc and Fannie if he could keep them moving.

But a hollow explosion rang out. Cheffal, standing in the center of the bridge, had fired a pistol into the air. All movement stopped. Bettoc's head snapped up, and he slid off of Fannie. Before George could stop him, he was half-running, half-staggering toward the bridge, calling out his elephant's name as he went: *Zulu, Zulu, Zulu.*

This time, Cheffal himself took charge. He met Bettoc on the road, dragged him into the woods and around the elephant, and across the bridge.

The elephant turned.

Now the men resumed their coercion: screaming, cursing, throwing rocks, provoking the elephant with hooks and whips.

Zulu put one foot on the bridge. Bettoc screamed. The elephant took another step forward, and another, lumbering, slow, until it reached the middle of the bridge, where it looked, for a second or two, as if it might gain the other side. All of them held their breath. The elephant turned its massive head around and held its tusks out in the air over the water swirling downstream below it. It made no noise now. The black eyes, calm as ever, seemed to be looking not down, but at them all. Then the arches gave a warning squeal as the metal buckled under all that weight. The surface of the bridge shivered briefly, and the whole structure collapsed into the gorge.

When he was released from prison after serving ten years for the destruction of H. C. Hutherford's property, it is hard to imagine that George Mattie would not have gone first to the home of that aunt in Albany. She knew where he had been. Elderly now, she offered him her small house for the night—not long to suffer the quiet boy she remembered, who left a room without a trace, as if he had never been there. But what he had once done like a thief, weeding the small garden or throwing a tub of laundry water out the back door, now carried the air of a favor. She began to listen for his step. Days passed. She knew he would not stay for long and tried to prolong his visit by cooking foods she thought he would like, stewed chickens and pies full of strawberries she picked herself. These he ate, slowly and deliberately, and thanked her.

She didn't ask him to leave, but he did, saying that he thought he would spend some time in the Shawangunk Mountains downstate. A few days after he had gone, she found a few belongings which he had left behind: a small aluminum bell, a handful of buttons, his straw hat. She never heard from him again.

Close to the Body

We used to throw trash bags out of the window at the second-floor landing, try to hit the big mouth of the Rubbermaid can down below.

And we would go to the supermarket, the Stop & Shop off I-95, in the middle of the night and forget what we meant to buy. Prowl up and down the aisles for ten minutes, twenty, thirty, startle limp-eyed stock workers out of their reveries with questions, pick up some tamarind nectar or Fontina cheese just to see what the hell it tasted like.

Or head over to the Jazz on the Square concerts and catch Tito Puente on a summer tour or a Manhattan Transfer knockoff from the local music circuit. Sun hot as hell, and the two of us spooned up with Ricky in the beach chair and me on the ground using his legs for armrests. Sweating like pigs and sharing a two-liter bottle of Nehi grape because we'd observed the rule against alcohol. Hanging out through all the sets, a fight or two, a couple of encores, and the draining of the crowd into the streets after it was all over. Used to.

From where I lie now in the dark, Ricky's back to me where he sits at the edge of the bed, his light-brown skin looks black and his white T-shirt seems to float free of his neck and arms. It's a screen where I play back the memories of happier times before this past year, but all in pantomime. No words. Words take too much energy.

Ricky twists around, stares, trying to see me. He knows I'm awake. Can he feel the pictures moving across his body?

"Mar," he says. "You can't just stay in here in the dark all the time like this."

I'm not just lying here, I could tell him. But instead, "I see the new doctor tomorrow" is what I say.

My first visit to Dr. Hamshell is at 2 P.M. the next day, a Friday. We sit across from one another in the chilly cube of an exam room with pastel-green walls and an orange exam bed while she leafs through my thick manila medical file.

"So, what can I do for you?" Dr. Hamshell asks, patting back a wisp of her gray-blond hair and flashing me a forced smile.

By now I understand that this question is not the absurdity it appears to be, so I don't answer, "Cure me." I did the first time, to a bearded internal medicine specialist who rocked back on his little stool and gargled out laughter at what he took to be a clever quip. For Dr. Hamshell I carefully recite my symptoms over the past months and end with a brief account of the few useless drugs and therapies I have tried.

"And you're still having the, ah . . ." She stops, leafs some more. "The muscle and joint pain, and the fatigue?"

"Yes."

"Nothing showing up in the tests here."

"I know."

"You've seen a lot of doctors for this," she says flatly.

"Yes."

"They haven't been much help."

I'm surprised by her remark. None of the other doctors spoke of their predecessors, either favorably or critically, and I have grown used to all of them turning shadowy as they passed out of my life, as if they had been merely casual visitors, like the Adventist people sticking leaflets in my front door.

"Not much," I say slowly.

She nods, stands up, and tells me she will do a physical exam now. She pokes around, tests my reflexes, makes me walk on tip-toe, checks my strength, asks me a few questions. When she listens to my heart and lungs with her stethoscope, I smell a faint perfume of soap and alcohol rising from her skin. It takes her only a few minutes to finish, then she sits back down on her stool.

For a moment Dr. Hamshell doesn't speak. Her hands rest on

the file folder on her lap, and her lips purse as if they are being drawn into her thoughts. She's the age I think of as motherly now that I am nearly thirty, but her soft crow's-feet and large glistening forehead and dry planar cheeks suggest nothing of anybody's mother in the presence of her stiff white lab coat. We are staring at one another. It is the oddest of moments, because I have no idea why she is regarding me this way, and yet I am loathe to take my eyes away for fear of missing something from this woman, this doctor who barely knows me.

"You look tired," she finally announces.

The odd feeling vanishes. This is as familiar as her opening question, and I understand it too. She is not telling me what I already know, nor is she trying to remind me of how bad I feel. She is merely thinking out loud, as if I am not here. So I say nothing.

"Try to relax, you'll feel better," she says. "Here. Like this." She makes fists, presses her arms against her chest. "Scrunch yourself up, even your legs." She folds herself up into a fetal position with her feet drawn up onto an upper rung of the stool. With her head down, she continues talking, and her voice comes through muffled. "Hold it like this a second or two, then release." And she spreads out like a hatching chick, arms in the air, legs as wide as her skirt will allow. Her head tips way back, and her mouth falls open. "And when you relax, try to think about something pleasant," she says. "A happy memory."

"A happy memory."

"Yes. Visualize it."

"That's an idea. I'll try that. Thank you so much."

She looks at me aslant as she picks up a clipboard from the counter, but leaves it at that. She says she'd like to run some tests, and for a few moments she writes on a sheet that looks like some of those I've taken to labs for bloodwork. I wait in the sterile, pastel silence as her pen scrabbles across the paper. She rises suddenly, mumbling something about grabbing a prep sheet, and slips out of the room. As I wait for her, I feel a creeping regret about the wisecrack I made, and sitting there in my paper gown I begin to formulate apologies in my head. *I'm sorry, Dr. Hamshell. I haven't been myself lately. It's not like me to be so rude . . .* By the time the door opens again, I've started to shiver in the paper gown. A small, child-like woman in a nurse's uniform steps in and says, "Oh, heavens, you're not dressed yet? You can come on up front now, honey." And then she, too, is gone.

Sleeping is like falling down into one of those whitish, oil-slicked puddles that you only find off the edge of a city curb. When I was a kid I used to jump over them. Who knew what would happen if I stepped in? What if it wasn't just two inches deep? Now I know that it's a long slide down through water so heavy with runoff that it's useless to try to struggle out. Useless, but impossible not to.

When I float up this Sunday morning, more tired than I was the night before, I can tell it's very early. Ricky lies breathing gently beside me. I crawl out of bed without waking him.

Out in the hall, a shard of paint crisps away under my hand and falls on the floor. This stops me in my tracks, makes me think about getting the Elmer's and gluing it back in place. The house is old, in need of renovations that Mrs. Poole, the landlady, has no intention of making. On cold winter nights the pipes clank forlornly and the baseboards creak, but during the summer the decay becomes silent and the place is as quiet as an empty church. Sometimes I think both of us, Ricky and I, live a little more noisily, slap pots on the stove and slam cabinets shut, just to compensate. I slip into the studio and turn on the desk lamp on my drafting table.

Here, until a few months ago, I did my illustrations. Interesting stuff, the kind you can't do properly on a computer. Trees in elevation, the delicate branch patterns of their canopies carefully exposed. A late-1700s blunderbuss with an engraved stock. The face of a child in REM sleep. I remember all too clearly just what is in the messy pile scattered across the tabletop, and in what state of incompletion. And how I finally weakened, hunched there over my illustrations, and gave in to the relief of codeine-laced capsules, three times a day, that blurred the fine details of the trees and guns and babies just as effectively as they did the pain. On top lies a pink cutaway of a lung, the alveoli exposed like grapes on a stem. I pick it up, and then pick up another, and another, until I can place a neat pile of sheets on a corner of the table.

For a few moments I stare at it. I can't hear Ricky breathing, and I can't hear the house even though I know its inaudible processes. On the old recliner next to the table are scattered magazines, mail, and newspapers that have been lying there long enough to collect a patina of dust. I sift out the magazines and stack them in the closet, throw away the newspapers, and sort through the mail until all the junk lies atop the mound in the wastebasket. Then I bag up the mound and drag it out to the kitchen, where I take a fresh trash bag from under the sink. Back in the studio I stare at the bookshelves, my table with its wood surface now visible, the old light sconce in the shape of cupped hands on the wall. And the semblance of my old quarters, like a kind of half-hidden logic, compels me as strongly as any hunger or thirst could. I dust the blinds with an old T-shirt of mine and then open them to let in the first light the room has seen since spring. When the dust settles, I sweep the floor and carry two panfuls of grit and dust balls to the kitchen trash. While I'm in the kitchen, I take the bucket from under the sink, fill it halfway with steaming water, add Pine Sol, the closest thing I can find to window cleaner, and carry it back to the studio with a sponge.

Later, seized up into a ball on the recliner, I hear Ricky come in. He stops just inside the doorway, leaves again, and then quickly comes back with a glass of water and two Tylenols with codeine, one of which I greedily swallow dry.

"Drink some water," he says.

"I don't want it," I tell him.

I grab for his hand with the other pill and my own lurches way off target, knocking my neat pile of drawings onto the floor. Ricky sighs, gives me the pill, and squats where the drawings have landed.

"Leave them alone, Ricky," I say.

Wordlessly, he gathers up every sheet, straightens the pile, and puts it back in place.

During my next visit to Dr. Hamshell, she tells me the latest round of tests has turned up nothing. Then she jumps up and ducks out of the room to get something. My file lies open on the counter, and I slide down from the exam table to look at it. It must be some kind of masochistic curiosity, I tell myself, that drives me to look at test results which she has told me are all within normal ranges. Sed rate, CK, chem screen, ANA, she said, T3, T4, TSH, all of it fine. Everything fine. This, she told me at the beginning of our appointment, was good news because it showed that "nothing serious is wrong."

There is a slight, cold wind drifting down from a ceiling vent over the counter. The pages in the file are attached by metal holders in a pair of holes punched through their tops. Some of the pages are photocopies of previous test results, reproduced so badly they are illegible. The letters and numbers of more than one run off the edge of the page. The graininess of others blacks out whole blocks of print. One page 2 lacks a page 1. A clunk at the door makes me jump, but whoever it is passes by without entering. I flip through reports by doctors. One says that I am an only child, which, when I think of my sisters, makes me laugh, though I stifle it quickly. Another says, "Patient admits to being accident proan" and I stand there staring at this invention for some time, mired in the word "admits" and all its criminal connotations. Then I flip ahead to Dr. Hamshell's notes, which I am sure will be accurate. The first page gives my age as thirty-eight. I smile, shake my head at the silliness of it. Nobody could believe that, could they? It must be a typo, a minor glitch of no consequence. Like "proan."

The door opens, and Dr. Hamshell steps in. Her lips draw back in a smile. I settle myself on the exam bed, and she positions herself between me and the file. Faced with her cool presence, the sharp, precise way she has swung herself into place, the lab coat and stethoscope and roomful of paraphernalia she commands, I let the question about the mistake in my age melt back down my throat. She has her hands clasped behind her, and she is staring at me again. I feel myself lean slightly forward.

"I've had some good results with this," Dr. Hamshell says, holding out a small paperback. "With patients with problems like yours."

I am thinking, *you just told me you hadn't found the problem*, but my hand has already taken the book and I look down at it without speaking. On the cover, a man and a woman roll around on a beach with a golden retriever and two children. Water laps gently in the background. There's no title on the cover, no text on the back, and for an absurd moment I wonder whether it is all pictures, a book for small children. The door clicks. Dr. Hamshell turns on her way out and tells me it's from the Patient Resource Library, keep it as long as I need to. Then she shuts the door behind herself.

Finally I locate the title on the spine: *Healing Spirit, Healing Heart: Rediscovering the Healer Within.* Well. If this is part of the price of getting to the bottom of things, I will play along with Dr. Hamshell, I decide. I slip the book into my purse, gather my clothes and get dressed, but when I am done my clothes feel all wrong, as if I have put them on backwards or gotten the buttons out of sync. I try to tug and straighten them back to their usual fit as I walk out to the front desk. The few nurses there drop their professional demeanor and stare at me as I pass.

That evening, Ricky and I have piperade for dinner, an omelet-like dish with eggs and peppers and tomatoes that my vegetarian cookbook tells me comes from the Basque region of Spain. While swirling the ingredients in a skillet, I could not make myself forget how gelatinous the raw eggs had looked fresh out of the shell. On my plate, however, they look like yellow flesh.

Ricky's still wearing the dress shirt and tie he went to work in this morning, though the tie is at least loosened around his neck. Some work thing is on his mind, I can tell by the way he eats. His head stays down while he chews, and his brushy auburn hair looks in need of a trim, which I am thinking of mentioning to him when he looks up suddenly, ready to talk.

"I had to fire somebody today," he says. "One of the tellers."

"Drugs?" I ask. "Or somebody dipping into the till again? Or did somebody finally get a little more creative for a change?"

At the branch he manages, these are constant nuisances, even with cameras all over the place that faithfully record every movement of people and money in the bank. Sometimes Ricky will say he caught something interesting on Candid Camera that day. Today, though, he ignores my joking.

"A stabbing," he says. "With a ballpoint pen." He looks at me. "What did the doctor say today?"

"A stabbing? Well, who? What for?"

"Mimi Georgias, we'd just hired her. Got mad at a customer and stuck a pen in his shoulder. Not a serious wound, but she had to go." He drives his fork into his piperade with a *clank,* and I know he is through with this. "Dr. Hamshell have anything for you?"

I could say yes, since I brought the book home with me and it is lying on top of the dresser in our bedroom. And then again I could say no. *Since ancient times,* the first page said, *the wisest among us have known that potions and powders and knives are not the best cure for illness. When the spirit is unleashed, no disease can prevail.*

Ricky chews slowly, waiting for my answer.

"What did he say," I ask, "that got her so angry?"

Ricky shrugs. "Nobody heard. Nobody knows." He gets up and goes into the kitchen for seconds, but when he comes back I see I was mistaken, that he has finished with dinner. He sits down, stretches out his long, lanky frame in the chair, and sits with his eyes closed behind the wire-rimmed glasses that make him look like an accountant. Sometimes I wonder how I came to be married to him.

Then he says, his voice tired, "Nothing, right?"

And the wondering seems silly.

"Nothing," I say.

That evening, I carry the half-read book out the back door into the rain. In the dark it takes some work to grope my way down the stairs and over to the place where we keep the trash cans. The overhead light is out, and Mrs. Poole has sent nobody to repair it in the two weeks since I phoned her to say that a new bulb did not fix the problem.

When I find the Rubbermaid can, I pull the lid and it pops off with enough force to send me reeling back a step. The wet leaves of the maple saplings growing along the border between Mrs. Poole's property and the house next door slap me in the face. I step away from them, in a hurry to finish my task, and realize that my hands are empty. I can't remember what I did with the book.

Did I leave it inside? It's too big for any of my pockets. When I turn to go back inside for it, I feel it scrape against my stomach inside my shirt. Yes, I remember now. I put it there, this book I was taking out to the trash, to keep it dry.

I shake my head. It makes no sense, protecting a book I mean to throw away.

I yank the book out of my clothing and squash it down into the trash can. My breath, in the cool, humid air, spirals up around my face. I yank some leaves off the maples and smash them down on top of the book. Still, I'm not ready to replace the lid, and I pull some garbage, a pizza box, a milk carton, something as slimy as the piperade, and a wad of cellophane, out of an adjacent can and mash it on top of the book. Between the dark and my billowing breath, I can hardly see a thing. I wedge the lid on tightly.

Summer goes by slowly, as if it is evaporating into the air a breath at a time. Dr. Hamshell is on vacation, but the results of the most recent round of tests she ordered trickle in with numbing regularity. I don't get the actual data, just brief, form-letter notices someone on her staff fills out in green ink and mails to me once a week or so. *Dear Patient,* they begin. All of them, even the ones where the writer has neglected to fill in the names of the tests, report the same thing: *No abnormalities detected.*

In July headaches set in, big blooms that press against the inside of my head so hard I can barely believe they are invisible things. In the bathroom I peer into the mirror, looking for some mark they have left on me, dents in my forehead, discolorations of my skin betraying the disturbance below. But there are none.

As I spend more and more time huddled in the bedroom, avoiding the bright light that exacerbates the headaches, the days should begin to blur. But they do not. In the quiet house I can hear everything going on in the street outside. In the mornings there are rattlings of keys and gunnings of motors as the neighbors leave for work. The children next door, liberated from school, chase up and down the street after one of their number on a battered bike, and clattering buoyed by laughter marks each pass they make by my window. Cabs honk in impatient bursts, other drivers in long, annoyed howls. After sundown the traffic eases, and the voices of people strolling by replace its rumble.

Eventually I abandon dinners to Ricky, and he fixes meals for the two of us without complaint. It's always been one of his charms that he knows basil from oregano and that he wipes up spills behind himself. He's a real kitchen man. One night I try to beg off dinner, which is nothing but hamburgers anyway, but he keeps at me until I sit down at the table. The first bite is a palette of flavors.

"Marla," he says after a while, "it's time to try another doctor." He puts down his hamburger, rubs his temples. "This one isn't helping you."

I don't want to discuss this with him, so I keep chewing. In the dim light, there seem to be shadows under his eyes.

"Maybe if Dr. Hamshell doesn't work out," I say.

He puts his fingers in a pyramid on the table, the way he does when he's trying to be patient. For him Dr. Hamshell has already not worked out. But I have seen so many doctors by now that I cannot imagine starting yet another round of questionings and pokings and proddings and drawings of blood, and I don't want to hear his lucid, clear-eyed arguments for doing so. I know it is childish, even irrational, to stick my head in the sand this way, as irrational, perhaps, as what I actually do want just now: an hour with Mrs. Conklin, whom until this moment I have despised. The doctor who sent me to her for physical therapy thought I had arthritis, and the exercises he prescribed only made me worse, but neither of these concerns me now. Those hands of Mrs. Conklin's, cold as refrigerated carrots, so very dry you might let her touch you anywhere and not feel invaded, those hands are what I need. Moving my arms up and down, turning me right and left, with such a calibrated regularity that only her hands remained after a while and the rest of her melted into the taupe walls, except, of course, for her voice playing back instructions: *When rising from a chair, put the weight on the better knee. Stay off the feet as much as possible. When doing chores, keep the arms and the hands close to the body.* The knee, the feet, the hands. It is as if we are discussing constellations in the night sky, seen at a great distance away.

"You look better," says Dr. Hamshell.

I've just told her about the headaches, and this is her response. I'm struck dumb by it. What is she talking about? My clothes fit so loosely I look like a badly wrapped gift these days, my hair is so tangled I can do nothing but wind it into camouflaging scarves. She herself looks exactly the same as she did before her vacation, her stockinged legs the color of milk, her face serene around the gray eyes.

"Well, I don't feel any better," I finally manage, and my voice sounds whiny and insistent in the air of that room.

"Recovery is not an overnight thing," Dr. Hamshell says. "It's a process that takes time and effort."

"Yes, yes, I know that," I reply, "but—"

"It's not just a matter of pushing a button or flipping a switch and making everything all right. Because sometimes, as much as we want there to be, there are no magic buttons. Sometimes there are no easy fixes. We have to look within ourselves."

She closes my file and drops it, without looking, on the counter behind her.

Her steady gaze is too much for me, and I look away, at my hands, at the chrome border of the footrest, the black seams between the squares of the blue and gray linoleum. It all starts to blur. I cannot gather the questions I had planned to ask her, nor my memories of these past few months, nor even, anymore, my own thoughts. I cannot even pull myself up straight.

"I'm not crazy," I say, and the dry rasp of my own voice repels me.

"I didn't say you were, " Dr. Hamshell says. "You see, that is exactly the kind of thinking that I am talking about."

When the taxicab drops me off at the house, I rush to the door and fumble so maddeningly with the key that I want to scream. Then the lock opens, and I go immediately to the bathroom, where I strip off all my clothes even though I took a shower only a few hours ago. The hot stream provides no relief, and hasn't for a long time, yet I stand there like a stone as the water temperature, another thing Mrs. Poole has neglected, flutters wildly up and down on its own.

Then I happen to look at the clear plastic shower curtain dotted with water droplets, and I see what I used to enjoy, thinking myself the only person in the world who would notice it: a thousand black dots, each of them a perfect refracted miniature of the Vermeer print hanging on the wall. A thousand perfect replicas. When I was a child I spent hours trying to get the world down so perfectly, drawing over and over again a rock or a dead bird, whatever I found. And my mother, who wanted a dirty, romping child like her other girls, would yell for me to put that paper down and get inside and at least help her with the dishes if all I was going to do was sit around parked on my butt all the livelong day. Whatever it was I sought to capture might never have been there at all. Maybe she had been right. I close my eyes on the field of Vermeers. It has become nothing more than a mute and common disappointment that opens onto nothing better.

Ricky asks me when my next appointment with Dr. Hamshell falls, and when I tell him it is two months away, he puts his hands on his hips and asks, Why so long? He follows me from the living room into the bedroom and back into the kitchen, where we face one another from opposite corners of the tiny room. Another awkward silence fills the air between us, and I am almost sure he is examining me for signs of anger which it frustrates him not to find. But I am feeling light today, perhaps because I have lost so much weight, and I just stare back at him.

He takes a scrap of paper from his pocket and smooths it between his long fingers.

"You just happen to have some doctors' names," I say flatly.

"Marla, look," he says, rubbing his eyes, "I know how hard this is."

"No you don't."

He looks at the floor for a moment, the paper dangling in his hands. "You're right, I don't. But I do know," he says, and pauses the way he does when he is being especially careful with his words, "what those two months are."

I lean back against the counter.

He stops waiting for me to ask. "Nothing. Two months of nothing. I bet this doctor, this, this Dr. Hamshell, is not going to do a damn thing in that time, is she?"

"This is not just a matter," I say, "of clearing checks or making loans, Ricky."

He frowns. "What is that supposed to mean?"

"I'm going to lie down," I say, and leave.

He follows me down the hall to the bedroom, where I step in and swing the door half-closed.

"Marla," he says, "wait a minute."

"Ricky," I say, "I am not a child."

He sighs and backs off a step. His hand wads the slip of paper into a lump in his pocket, and he tips a bit to lean against the wall.

"When was the last time you changed your clothes, Mar?" he asks softly.

Since he started doing our laundry I've lost track of some things. I've slept in this sweatshirt and these jeans a few nights, I am sure, but I don't know how many. But I can smell the staleness of the clothes now that he's drawn my attention to them.

"Try to wake me in a couple of hours," I tell him, and shut the door.

I crawl into bed fully dressed and wait for sleep.

A few days later we are flying down the Merritt Parkway. It's not a ride I wanted to take, but I have agreed to "get out for a little air" with Ricky to placate him. It's a route I know well, and I don't bother watching the tedious scenery go by.

For a while he tells me news about his bank, and I listen with half my attention. The Georgias woman is back working at the bank because the man she attacked would not press charges. Another teller is pregnant. There is talk about opening a branch in Lloyd's, a discount warehouse store, but there is also talk of a merger with another, larger bank.

"Things have been a little crazy since they let Ed go," he says.

Ed Tennant is the assistant manager of Ricky's branch, the one who takes care of old men who walk in wanting to cash ten-year-old checks and children cramming Tootsie Rolls into the ATM. "When did this happen?" I ask.

"About a month ago. Restructuring."

"A month ago? Who's been covering his work?"

"Me, mostly. He saw it coming, though. Already had some leads. Way back at year-end he was saying we all ought to be looking around."

"Is your job in danger?"

Ricky laughs. "Yes. Let's stop for a few minutes at that new mall out here." He signals and turns off at the exit. "It's supposed to have an aquarium or something in it."

I stare at him. "Ricky, why didn't you tell me?"

"I did," he says mildly.

He makes a sharp turn at the end of the ramp and then another into the mall's parking lot, where he pulls us into a space near an entrance. He squeezes my hand. "Don't worry about it," he says, and smiles, and then he is out of the car and around my side, opening the door for me.

Inside the mall, Ricky gives me his arm and I take it and follow where he leads me. He points out things to me, and I look and make some sort of noise of recognition, and he seems satisfied. The shock of what he told me in the car passes quickly, and after a while I am just walking, and I am light again. Ricky stops us.

"Well," he says, "this is it."

"What?"

"The aquarium."

In front of where we stand, small glass tanks sit on either side of carpeted platforms placed like stairs ascending over a pool with fountains. But when we move closer, we see that the tanks are empty and merely serve as backboards for displays of mounted insects under glass covers. There's a sign next to a potted plant saying this exhibit, "Insects of the World," will remain for several months while the aquarium is "under construction."

We step up onto the first platform for a look. The first bug has enormous black pincers sprouting from where its head should be.

"Let's go," I tell Ricky.

"Already?" he says. "Aren't you a little curious?"

I sigh, look at a few more, but they are even more hideous than the first. One looks like it is made of sticks. I ignore the labels that name them. Another is green and fist-sized, with overgrown legs thickened by something like fur. I turn away.

"It's the stairs, isn't it?" Ricky, beside me, says.

And before I can answer that it is not, he has lifted me into his arms and everything around me shifts crazily, the floor falls away, the ornamental rafters in the ceiling lean at an insane angle. "Ricky!" I try to say; but my breath is just a gasp, and I grab onto his arms to try to restore my equilibrium. But he moves, crossing the platforms, mounting the stairs, and I lose my last bit of purchase, and lights and plants and beams and bits of sky whirl around me like debris in a wind devil, and I hold on tighter until my head drops back and laughter, my own laughter, bubbles up out of my open mouth. I let go of Ricky. He is not even there. I don't know where I am, only that I am rising, flying, as I should have let myself rise long ago, and in the blur the hideous insects become beautiful, beautiful colors.

But Ricky doesn't understand, and suddenly his face looms over me and his mouth clamps down over mine in a heavy kiss. And everything stops, and I fall back.

That night, instead of sleeping in the bedroom, I drag a pillow and an old blanket into the studio. Ricky stands in the hall and asks me what I am doing, and I snap at him, What does it look like I'm doing? He doesn't answer, just stands silently in the shadows and watches me.

The recliner is a big one, its nubbly plaid upholstery pilled and shaved by age. It's comfortable for reading, but by morning I am even stiffer and achier than usual from not being able to turn and stretch. But my sleep has been so dappled and frothed with dreams that I hardly notice, and in spite of the discomfort I try to doze a little more.

When I come out and wander into the living room, I find a knot of sheets and pillows wound into the cushions of the couch. Ricky's alarm clock sits on its side on an end table, and the television is on but muted. I turn it off. I decide not to think about any of it, whatever Ricky has been doing. But in the bedroom the bed is unmade, its sheets dragging on the floor instead of being tucked into the hospital corners Ricky favors, and my mind wanders through the apartment the way I imagine he did in the night.

The next night I sleep in the recliner again and though it is painful just to get myself out of it in the morning, I understand how good it is for me to be there, free of the tensions and pressures of the bedroom, the distractions that used to cloud my mind. Ricky insisted that we switch sides of the bed every six months so the mattress would wear evenly. He would press himself against me in his sleep, and sometimes, on cool nights that marked the cusp between two seasons, he would slide over and rest his head against my side, on my ribs, and leave me lying awake for hours. Now, when I venture out of the studio, the morning is like a fresh, new emergence.

I spend a lot of time in the recliner, and now, in mid-August, the sounds from outside, the kids and their bike, the neighbors and their horns, fade away into the quiet of Mrs. Poole's old house. Even by day I keep the room bathed in darkness. And I wonder why it took me so long to let this quiet enter me.

One night something awakens me. It is not the television, for I know that Ricky keeps it low, or turns off the sound, so as not to wake me. I roll over, my hand falls into a hollow where my jeans, now far too large, gap away from me, and I feel a small bulge against my hip. Half asleep, I probe with my fingers until what I find jolts me fully awake. Some sort of nodule lies between my fingers and my pelvic bone.

My dream of flying over the city, shattered by the interruption of my sleep, vanishes in the dark as completely as what was never there. I sit up, unzip my pants, and feel for it again, expecting to find that it was only a tangle of clothing. But it is still there.

I tell myself it is nothing, to go back to sleep, but my heart pounds. So I drag myself up and stagger to the bathroom, where I turn on the light over the medicine cabinet. The illumination is so bright that, for a moment, the mirror in front of me reflects only a blankness where my face should be. My jeans drop around my ankles, and my face comes into focus. The person staring back, with its tangle of hair like a swath of matted fur, its eyes ringed by skin that looks caramelized, dirty around the neck and fingernails, cannot be me.

Neither can the bulge my fingers expose when I pull down my panties: a gumball-sized, ugly, carbuncular knot that looks like a brown scarab trying to work its way into my skin. *Not me,* I tell myself, *this thing is not me,* and I throw open the cabinet and scratch around the shelves until I find the matte knife we keep there to trim loose caulk in the shower. I flick the button, and the blade unsheathes. It is cold for a minute when I press it against my skin. But when I grab the nodule to hold it steady to the blade, it is soft, warm, not the rock-hard growth I expect, and I drop the knife in the sink. It clatters and comes to rest blade-down in the drain.

My shoulder hits the door as I back out of the room, and a shower of needles erupts inside it. All I can think of, now, is getting back to the sanctuary of my studio. My hips grind as I creep back down the hall, and I run one hand along the wall to steady myself. Another step and I am at the recliner, and I let myself fall into it.

Ricky is there.

He must have come in to wait for me and fallen asleep, and amazingly, he seems to be sleeping still, for he says nothing to me, just breathes evenly. Jammed against him as I am, I am sure I will wake him if I get up again, and yet I cannot stay here, and I don't know what to do. He turns a little, and his hand slides over my hip. I push it away quickly, as gently as I can. But his arm falls across me again, his hand right on the nodule, and before I can do anything, he whispers, "I know."

His hand rests there until I calm down enough for my breathing to fall into sync with his. Then he takes my hand and pulls it upward, over my breasts, to my shoulder. And there, in the curve of my collarbone just under my shirt, my fingers touch another of my small lumps. He leaves my hand there, pressed against me, for a moment, until he is sure that I have felt it. Then he pulls my hand away and down my side, just slightly behind my back. And I reach for the next one that he will show me. He doesn't shrink away at all, doesn't say another word. He is as warm and deep against me as my own blood.

And I understand.

SOUVENIR

Gail Henderson, her eyes shut, steers the white rented Ford Tempo along a weaving path over the pavement of a two-lane Florida highway. The more she tries to straighten its course, the more it lurches from side to side, and it is only when she feels the car kick up a spray of gravel at the right shoulder that she begins to get her bearings and a degree of control. Finally she gets the car to follow a jerky but relatively straight line down what she thinks is the right lane of the road.

"There you go," says Lucille Green, her best friend, from the passenger seat. "You're in the lane, now. You drive just about as good with your eyes closed as you do with 'em open."

They both giggle, and Gail, wound up by the game of driving blind and the odd disembodied quality of Lucille's voice, almost shouts her reply. "Cille, we go and bust up some cracker's orange grove, you're the one who's gonna pay for it! You hear me?"

For a moment Gail hears no answer, and she wonders why she is doing this. The game, after all, is Cille's concoction and finally now, with the wheel clutched in her sweaty hands and her heart pounding wildly, it occurs to her that it would have made more sense for Cille to have taken the first turn. At least she thinks so.

"Quit worrying, Gail. You worry too damn much. Steer a little left."

Gail turns the wheel slightly.

There's a rustling beside her which Gail takes to be Cille moving around, and then, in the next instant, Cille is yelling at her and pulling at the wheel.

Gail opens her eyes. In a flash she takes in the scrubby land, a few palmettos, a ragged orange grove off to the right, a scattering of shacks collapsing in on themselves farther back from the road, and the oncoming van, an old VW microbus painted over in a lusterless shade of black. She wrenches the wheel, and the car leaps to the right, spins a full circle and a half, and comes to rest with its rear tires cupped in the sandy dirt at the side of the road. Neither Gail nor the other driver, who is now out of sight, has even blown a horn.

Gail lets go of the wheel, not in relief but because her hands are shaking so badly that she has to thrust them between her knees. But her knees are shaking too. She looks over at her friend. Cille is small and keeps her hair trimmed neat and close to her scalp, a style that flatters her angular head but one which Gail would never try. She wears cut-off jeans and a black T-shirt that says, on the front, "You wouldn't understand." On the back, "It's a Noo Yawk thang." Her bare arms and legs, when the sun hits at the right angle, seem to throw back an almost copper light.

"Damn, girl!" Cille says in a breathless voice. "Are you crazy?"

"What do you mean, am *I* crazy?" Gail asks. "You started it!"

Cille gapes. "Well, Gail, you ain't supposed to *really* close your eyes, fool. It's just a game!"

Gail blinks. "Oh."

At the sound of this, they both are taken with a fit of convulsive giggling. After a minute they wind down, look at each other, and burst into laughter again.

When they finish, Gail wipes her hands on her starchy, yellow camp shirt, which is already damp with sweat, and then on her white shorts, which she no longer cares about soiling, and says, "Why do I listen to you?"

Cille smiles and tucks her legs back up under her. "We gonna sit here all day?"

Gail takes out a cigarette, snaps a lighter and makes three wobbly passes before managing to ignite anything with it. "You just had to get us off the interstate, have a look around," she says.

She restarts the car and pulls back out onto the road.

"That's what I get for letting you do the driving," Cille says in mock disgust. She opens the window as Gail's smoke swirls through the Tempo's interior and theatrically sucks fresh air through the crack. "And look at us now. Lost out in the middle of fucking Tropicana country."

After a while out on the same road, they switch positions. Lucille drives and Gail rides with a map spread over her lap and her feet propped awkwardly on the dashboard. Her mother would be giving her hell about getting them off. If she were there, anyway. Right now, she doesn't even know where Gail is.

A truck approaches, an old pickup with so much of its color washed away that it looks blue, slightly orange, or vaguely green depending on the angle from which it is seen. Its windows are down. A beat-up box on wheels, it bears a pair of rangy, shirtless blond men in its cab, their arms hanging from the windows.

"Well, looka hyeah," Cille drawls.

The driver has a cigarette dangling from his lips. Gail watches Cille stare into his face as the truck and their car draw closer together. She could tell Cille the engine was on fire, and Cille wouldn't hear it. Then the truck passes, close enough to make a *fwump* that shakes the car like something invisible bumping against it.

Another second, and the pickup is out of sight.

"Act like they own the whole damned road," Gail says, "don't they?"

But Cille doesn't acknowledge the remark at all. She sits up in the seat and cranes her neck, peering off into the distance down the road. Gail hasn't noticed until now that it is getting on toward evening, and although the day will stay light past eight o'clock, it's not a very fine or clear light anymore. Even with few shadows on the ground, the horizon blurs where the green and tan earth meet the blue sky.

"We need some gas," Cille says. "We're on empty."

"On *empty*?"

They had a quarter tank at least when Gail was driving. The last time she remembers looking at the gauge, anyway. She leans over and peers at the dashboard.

"Cille, we're not out of gas, that's the engine light."

Cille glances down and the light, shaped vaguely like an anvil, flashes off and on as if on cue.

"What the hell does that mean?"

Gail flops her head back on the headrest in exasperation. "Do I look like a mechanic? How should I know?"

"Look, don't have a baby," Cille says. "There's gotta be a way to get back on I-95 around here somewhere. We'll just get off at the next exit that has gas and stuff."

Gail pores over the map again, trying to pinpoint their location. The last thing she wants is to get stuck out in the middle of nowhere, to have to deal with some hayseed local mechanic who might tell them it's too late to work on the car, assuming he actually does know how to fix it. It's bad enough that they're probably nowhere near their destination. When they started out from SUNY New Paltz yesterday, they were planning to make it to Melbourne in two days' drive. Their few belongings, clothes and books, chairs and a couple of lamps, they'd left in a U-STOR-IT near the Thruway. Their summer jobs, Gail's as a girls' camp counselor, Cille's at a law firm in Queens, where she was from, wouldn't start for another week. The stress of finals was over, for a while they were free, and to convince themselves of it they meant to get as far away from New Paltz as they could.

It couldn't be Daytona, though. Cille dismissed the idea. She'd never been to Florida herself, or even out of the Northeast, Gail knew, but she'd heard that the place was nothing but white-kid party territory, during spring break and the rest of the year too. So they picked Melbourne and flew down I-95, daring any troopers to ticket them as they did 70, 80, even 90 m.p.h. for a while in Maryland. Somewhere in North Carolina, Gail thought about her parents getting worried and driving up to New Paltz to find her. It seemed kind of silly, not having mentioned the trip to her parents, turning off her voice mail so it wouldn't overflow and tip them off that she was gone. Hell, it was just a week in Florida. The worst she would have gotten were stupid warnings about sunstroke and alligators and not swimming too soon after a meal. Still, she enjoyed the slipping away. And the thinking about them wondering as they sat down to dinner, chewing on swordfish steaks her mother slathered with garlic butter and her father seared on the big gas grill he kept on the deck.

"We've got to find a garage that's open late," she tells Cille.

"Would you relax? Have one of your damn cigarettes or something." Cille gives her a smirk. "You just let old Cille do the driving."

A few miles down the road, past a low, one-story school and a lot of scrubby, fenced-in fields with nothing in them, there's a sign for I-95.

"Told you," Cille says.

Not until it is nearly dusk do they find an exit marked for gas and food. It's clear that they will not make it by dark to Daytona, much less Melbourne, so there is no longer a reason to hurry. The engine light has been off long enough to be forgotten. The May night, from what Gail can see through her window, does not look to be cooling off much even with the sun going down. There's no more shimmer of heat mirages, but the land looks parched.

They follow the arrows on the signs that point toward gas and food, ignoring the numbers of the routes and the names of the towns they reach. Not far from the interstate they find a Shell station, sprawling and clean, with enough pumps arrayed under canopies to accommodate eight or ten cars at once. Its lights sparkle against the dimming sky, which has taken on a metallic cast. Yellow potted geraniums, two per island, glow starkly in the bright light.

While Cille is inside, paying for gas, Gail finds a plastic bucket full of murky water and a squeegee next to one of the geraniums. She cleans off the front and rear windows and is working on the side ones when Cille comes back out.

"Little Miss Clean," Cille says, and laughs. "My card ain't working. We gotta use yours."

"You out of money?" Gail asks, stunned.

"Hell, no," Cille says, and waves off the idea. "It's just the magnetic strip, or maybe they got something fucked up at the bank. I'll call in the morning."

After they've gotten gas, they drive across the street to a truck-stop restaurant under a big neon sign that says "Pop Connors

Restaurants." It's large for the lonely spot it occupies, and there are more blue-aproned waitresses than customers inside. Even so, the hamburgers they order take a long time to arrive. Gail starts to feel languid with hunger. It helps little that the air-conditioning, even after dusk, is straining just to keep the room tepid. The waitresses pat their foreheads with white napkins as they wander by, looking off ahead of themselves so intently God himself might be beckoning. After twenty-five minutes of waiting, Cille gets up to track theirs down.

"She said a minute," she says when she comes back.

Gail nods and slouches in her side of their booth. Cille sets the table vibrating by tapping her foot rapidly. In a few minutes the waitress, a stout, older woman with prominent cheekbones and short reddish hair that would look punk on someone younger, brings the food. She asks if they want anything else, and when Gail and Cille say no, she puts the check on the edge of the table and leaves.

Gail watches Cille throw the woman a lingering glance. Her first mouthful of hamburger tells her that the food is cold, but she is ravenous by now and stuffs her mouth. Cille pokes the food with her fork and looks under the bun before she takes a bite and chews slowly.

"Pop Connors could use some cooking lessons," Cille says.

"Yeah." Gail makes herself eat more slowly. "This tastes like it's a week old."

"A week?" Cille says. "Try a month."

They both laugh, and Cille drains the rest of her soda. Gail sips some of her drink, an iced tea much sweeter than she's accustomed to. It makes her tongue feel thick. She catches the waitress, standing over at the register and talking to the cashier, looking over at her and Cille's table.

"I wonder who this Pop Connors is anyway," Cille says. "Is he like Roy Rogers or something? One of them singing cowboys who opens some restaurants?"

Gail has no idea. "I doubt he's even real."

"How do you know?"

"Like Ronald McDonald. He's probably made up."

"Then why don't they have his picture up anywhere? You know how they do that shit. They got Uncle Ben's face all over the damn box, like the man's personally back there in the kitchen fixin' up a mess of rice all nice and pretty like he's supposed to."

"Is he real?"

Cille looks disgusted. "Hell no he ain't real, Gail! That's the point."

She shoves her picked-over food aside, and Gail sits back in the booth and takes a long breath. In the recesses of her memory is a vague recollection that he was real, a rice grower somewhere or other, but she can't recall for sure and suddenly she's tired, too tired for this conversation. She'd like a cigarette, but when she feels around in her purse she finds the pack empty. She's gone through the whole thing in one day, far more than she usually smokes.

"I'll drive the rest of the way to Melbourne," she says.

Cille starts tapping again. "We ought to stay here tonight. They must have a motel or something around here."

The waitress is heading toward them, moving around corners as slowly as a bus, as if she is taking care with a great, dangerous bulk.

"They'll hold the room in Melbourne," Gail says. "We can check in late."

"I'm tired of being cooped up in that damned car."

"We already paid for the room in Melbourne."

Cille leans over the table. "So we call and cancel it."

"We can't cancel it after six o'clock," says Gail. "They'll charge us whether we show up or not." She knows this because she made the reservations.

"Oh yes I *can* cancel it after six. You watch me."

The waitress stops at the edge of their table.

"Y'all drivin' a white Ford?" she asks.

"Why?" asks Cille.

The waitress puts her hands on her hips. "Headlights is on, is all. Gonna kill your battery after a while."

"You get the bill," Cille says, sliding out of the booth. "I'll go check."

And before Gail can protest, she's past the waitress and heading for the door. The waitress smiles at Gail and heads off toward the back of the restaurant.

By the time Gail has paid the bill, left a tip, and made her way back out to the parking lot, Cille is in the car with the motor running. Gail climbs in the passenger seat.

"It's okay?" she asks Cille.

"No problem," Cille says, putting the car in drive.

Gail breathes a sigh of relief. Her watch says nine-thirty, time to stop messing around and get to Melbourne. The sky overhead is now a starless black dome lit only by the lamps of the Shell station and, farther away, a faint brightness at the ramps to the interstate.

"I told you I'd take care of it."

Gail frowns. "Take care of what?"

"The reservation. They canceled it, no charge. We're free."

"Goddamnit, Cille, I don't want to stay in some little backwater—"

"Oh chill *out*, will you? It's no big deal, okay? We'll get you all tucked in nice with your teddy bear and shit real soon. Then maybe I'll go see if there's something fun to do around here somewhere."

They pull back out onto the road and Gail watches the lights of the Pop Connors and the Shell recede behind them.

Not more than five minutes down the highway, roadside lights appear in the distance.

"See, I told you," says Cille. "You'll be getting your milk and cookies soon."

"Cille, would you knock it off?"

Gail wonders whether Cille is right, that they have been cooped up in the car for too long. Cille used to get smart-assed with her back when they didn't really know each other very well yet. That was sophomore year, when Cille transferred from City College to SUNY New Paltz. They wound up roommates in a suite for four in one of the drafty older dorm buildings with drab concrete walls and elevators that rarely worked. One night, when Gail was watching TV and Cille was waiting around for some friends she was supposed to go to a party with, they just fell into talking, mostly about what a sorry little hippie shithole New Paltz was. Funny thing was, they hadn't been able to stand each other before that.

"You need some cigarettes, right?" Cille says.

They're approaching a gas station with a convenience store attached. The place has only two pumps, but the store is huge, bigger than the Shell, with plate glass windows all around that reveal a sole occupant, a man behind the counter.

"No," says Gail. "I'll get some tomorrow."

But Cille pulls in anyway. The car rolls over the bumpy dirt lot and comes to rest with the front bumper almost kissing the low wall of the facade. The man looks up from a newspaper he's been reading. It is 9:47 P.M.

Cille turns off the engine. "We can ask about motels."

Gail doesn't move.

"What's wrong?"

"Nothing."

"You wanna wait out here, that's fine with me. It's your habit."

Cille is smiling, but Gail doesn't smile back.

"Cille, you're a pain in the ass sometimes, you know that?"

Cille laughs. "Maybe the old dude has a phone. You can call home."

Gail turns away and hurls open the door, but Cille grabs her arm before she can get out.

"You know I'm only playing with you, don't you, Gail?" she says, and in the dim interior of the car, Gail sees her smile fade away to a serious expression.

Gail doesn't say anything.

"Come on, Gail. You know I don't mean anything by it. Right?"

Gail examines her friend. Cille's staring at her out of those almond-shaped brown eyes, out of that pecan-shaded face of hers that never gets blemishes. If she grew a mustache, she'd still be pretty. Cille is . . . Cille, day in, day out, no change and no regrets. Cille pays her bills or she doesn't, she smokes or she quits, she lets a guy know she wants him or she tells him to get lost. Cille's her barometer, the little kick in the butt that tells her when she needs to hear it, "Gail, quit being so goddamned half-assed."

"Yeah," she says.

"All right."

Cille gives her a playful punch in the shoulder.

"So you with me?"

"Sure," Gail says, and they get out of the car, and they walk in.

Inside, once again, the air is wet with humidity. Gail feels herself almost panting. What is it with Floridians and their pathetic air conditioners? Haven't they figured out that something more heavy-duty than the Sears family special is needed to handle weather like this? She has never been so miserably hot. She would give anything for a sea breeze right now. But there is no relief here, just Cille picking out a bag of potato chips across the store, rows and rows of dented cans and dusty boxes in back, and shelves of ticky-tacky tourist junk up front. And behind the counter a man, neither young nor old, just worn leathery, sidling slowly back and forth as if he is searching for the best spot from which to keep an eye on them.

The trinkets are like the ones she's seen at every interstate rest stop. Hunks of driftwood with "Florida" painted across them, shells glued together to make figures, shells strung to make necklaces, shells in bottles, conch shells, cowrie shells, snail shells. Though she's not interested, she picks them up and fingers them as the man behind the counter watches out of the corner of his eye. She gives each one loving attention. Let him stare his eyes out of his head.

When she looks around, Cille catches her eye and holds up two bags, one of popcorn, one of pretzels. Gail shrugs, wanting none of either, and Cille puts the pretzels back and continues picking through the contents of the shelf. The man behind the counter shifts his attention to Cille, and Gail wanders to another table. The display is multilevel, with a shelf of glass holding an assortment of wooden souvenir boxes on top and an array of ceramic figurines below. Gail bends down for a better look, but her eyes haven't deceived her. The little figures are pitch-black people, bug-eyed things with head rags and red polka-dotted aprons and wet grins wide as the Mississippi.

Gail turns around to wave Cille over. *Would you look at this shit?* But Cille is absorbed in her search, and Gail changes her mind. Despite what Cille said when they got out of the car, she has a feeling, tonight, that it won't take much to get Cille started again. *Well what were you expecting, Gail? Harriet Tubman figurines? Don't you know where the fuck you are?* As a matter of fact, she doesn't know, and she's beginning to think Cille doesn't know either, just where her friend's bright idea has taken them. She knows well enough that this is Florida, where her family used to spend a week every year when she was a kid, where they keep Mickey Mouse and alligators, flowery Cypress Gardens and murky cypress swamps. Sea World with its laughing dolphins, and, here and there, behind all the tropical growth, lovingly restored as if it were a thing to be proud of, an old plantation house with a whistle walk out back. And a guide in goofy period costume, explaining with a smile about a slave boy whistling all the way from the kitchen to the house to prove he wasn't eating any of the master's food. They are in between, somewhere, she and Cille, and the feeling of being neither distinctly here nor there heightens the oppression of the heat and the tickle of sweat running down between her breasts.

Gail picks up one of the statuettes: a fat woman with her eyes smiled shut and a broom in her hands.

"*How* much?" says Cille loudly from across the room.

She's at the counter with a pile of stuff between her and the man.

"Eleven fifty," the man says, "even."

"For that? How much is this?"

"Three fifty."

"Three fifty! For a bag of popcorn? The sign said a dollar twenty-five!"

"That's for pretzels. Look, if you don't want it, don't buy it."

"If I didn't want it, I wouldn't be up here with it, would I?"

Gail can't see Cille's face, but she can tell that the man, who is hunching up his shoulders and breathing hard, is getting as angry as Cille. She could step in and break it up, drag Cille out of the place; Cille would yell a few insults on the way, but she would let Gail lead her away, and once Gail had her outside her anger would cool off shortly. It has happened before. Cille would mutter something, laugh, and be on to the next thing while Gail . . .

"I'm saying if y'all don't like my prices, y'all can shop somewheres else."

"Y'all who? Ain't nobody up here but me. Who's this 'y'all' you think you're talking to?"

The man's shoulders unclench, and he unballs his fists and spreads his hands on the counter, but Gail can see he's far from relaxed.

"You heard what I said."

Cille puts her hands on the counter too. "Oh, I see. Well, you know what?"

They stare at each other a second, but the man says nothing. Cille picks up the bag of popcorn and slaps it down on the counter between his hands.

"You can take your y'all-price popcorn and shove it up your ass!"

She turns and marches out the door. Once she's gone, the man doesn't turn his attention to Gail. He just picks through the things on the counter, as if each is suddenly very important to him. The mammy-thing in Gail's hand smiles up at her serenely. She's held it throughout the scene at the register, and her palm is now so slick that it threatens to slide out of her grasp and shatter on the red tile floor. She would like to let it. She has always been careful of things in stores, careful not to mess up displays, careful not to break things, but all of that seems ridiculous at the moment.

The man behind the counter finally shifts his gaze to Gail and keeps it there. Gail stares back, but it is not long before she looks away. She's never been able to stare like Cille, that laser-through-the-heart, fuck-you stare that rises above mere rudeness. No matter how angry she gets, something in her gives in. And she hates it, especially now.

Whaaaaaaaaaaaa! Cille is leaning on the horn.

The man behind the counter startles and knocks a bag of chips on the floor. They hit with a gentle *thwak* right before Cille blows the horn again. The man throws an irritated glance out the window at Cille.

By the time his eyes return to Gail, she is moving, pushing through the print-smeared plate glass door, out into the night.

Back on the road, Cille is a little wired.

"Maybe we ought to drive around a little, check this place out," she says, tapping a rhythm on the steering wheel with the knuckles of one hand.

"I thought you were tired of driving."

"Not anymore."

"Well I am," Gail says. "I want to check in and get some sleep and get out of here first thing in the morning, all right? So can we please find a motel?"

"Whatever you want. Just say where."

But "where" is the problem. There's not much along the road besides the gas station they have left, and nothing else is open. Then they come to an intersection with a larger, more promising road and turn toward lights in the distance.

"You believe that guy in the store?" Cille laughs. "He—"

Red and blue lights dance behind them. Gail looks in the side mirror at the police car in their wake and waits to see whether it will pull out and speed off in response to whatever call has set it in motion. It weaves slightly, then settles in tight on their bumper, and Cille grumbles and pulls over to the side of the road. The police car stops behind them, and a lone officer gets out and walks toward Gail and Cille's car.

He taps on the window. Cille rolls it down.

"License and registration."

Gail cannot see his face, which hovers out in the dark among the whooshing lights of passing traffic. The disembodied voice is so unreal that at first she doesn't heed it. Then Cille nudges her, and she opens the glove box and fishes out the rental contract.

Cille hands it and her license out the window.

"Step out of the car, please," the voice says.

Gail watches Cille's hands tense around the steering wheel. Then Cille surprises her by glancing at her briefly, with a frozen-eyed look that is new to Gail, before getting out of the car. It startles Gail so deeply that it is a moment before she thinks to try to listen to what is going on outside. But the whir of constant traffic, punctuated by occasional car or truck horn blasts, drowns everything out.

Cille's form is visible only as a darkness against the rushing head- and taillights. Gail leans closer to the open driver's window, straining to hear. Should she get out? It would probably be safest to just sit there. That's what she's heard is best, to stay put. Highway traffic was dangerous, cops in pull-over situations were nervous. And yet how can she sit there as if she has nothing to do with it? What she catches through the window, in bits and pieces, sounds like a swelling argument.

She opens the car door and steps out.

There are three people, not two, on the shoulder. Besides Cille and the officer—a stocky man in short sleeves—there is another man standing there. When the officer beckons her over and she approaches the group, she sees the man from the gas station convenience store.

"What's your name?" the cop says.

"Gail Henderson."

"This here your friend?"

"Yes."

"Where y'all headed?"

"I told you," Cille cuts in, "we're looking for a motel."

"Didn't I tell you to shut up?" the cop says.

Cille makes a noise of disgust and turns away.

"Now, where y'all going?"

"Melbourne," Gail replies.

"What y'all stop at Weber's for?"

He doesn't explain who Weber is. Gail understands that she is not a welcome visitor here, that she and Cille are not travelers who are going to be treated with patient indulgence. That clear-cut concretes are what the cop is looking for.

"Cigarettes," she says flatly.

Oddly, the day has finally cooled. It's not a drastic change, just a dissipation of the worst of the heat, a slight divergence from the Florida air she's grown used to that lets Gail finally breathe easier.

"Y'all take anything from Weber's?" the cop asks.

"Would you please tell him," Cille interrupts again, "that I do not steal—"

"Shut up!" the cop says. He turns back to Gail. "Well?"

"No."

The cop takes Weber by the arm and moves back toward the police car with him. They talk for a moment, then Weber returns to the police car and the cop comes back to where Gail and Cille are standing.

"He ain't pressing charges," the cop says.

"He ain't got a thing to be pressing charges for!" Cille replies.

The cop ignores her and continues speaking to Gail. "Cameron's Motel is right up the road, about three lights, on the left. Got that?"

"I can hear you fine," Gail says.

"Y'all be on your way first thing tomorrow."

"We weren't planning to vacation here."

He looks at her for a moment and then walks away without another word, leaving her and Cille standing next to their car on the shoulder.

"I'll drive," Gail says. "Come on, let's go."

When they find the motel and pay for their room, the last one available in the shabby, one-floor operation just off the highway, Cille is still complaining.

"Like he can just pull us over when he pleases or something."

"He had a complaint, Cille," Gail says.

She sits down on one side of the lumpy, queen-sized bed. There are cigarette burns in the bedspread, which is covered with pictures of seashells and tall, thin wading birds.

"From that peckerwood? Please! I left all his shit right there on the counter right under his nose. Now if I'm gonna shoplift something from the store, am I gonna be stupid enough to pick an argument with the man first?"

Gail unhooks her sandals and slips them off.

"I don't think so! No, he just figures 'Oh, I got a couple of Negroes loose in my store, sure enough one of 'em just gotta steal somethin'."

"Cille," Gail says.

When her friend looks, she unbuttons her camp shirt down to the waist, and the big-grinned mammy-thing with the red and white apron tumbles out onto her lap.

At first Cille doesn't understand. "What the—where'd you—"

She looks down at it, then back up at Gail's face.

"No, Gail—did you—oh *shit*, I don't believe it!"

Gail smiles.

"You had it on you when the cop pulled us over?"

"Yep."

"And you got out of the car?"

Gail nods, and Cille laughs with her hand clapped over her mouth.

"And you givin' him this 'I hear you fine' shit? Damn, girl, I can't believe you!"

Gail lets Cille ask her questions for a while, and she answers them, and they laugh over the answers. She's tired enough to fall over on the bed right then and there, but with Cille buzzing around her she is barely aware of it, or the lumpy mattress, or the stale smell of the room. Finally, while they're cracking up loudly, someone from the adjoining room pounds on the wall, and they pause, snicker, and start laughing again.

"You see that look he gave me at the counter?" Cille says.

"Yeah."

"That, what was his name?"

"Weber," Gail says.

"Yeah, Weber. I shoulda busted that bag of popcorn open."

"Really!"

"That'd give him something to be popping his eyes over."

"Sure would."

As Gail watches and listens, Cille replays the scene from the convenience store, then starts over and does it again, embellishing it a little, heightening her own fury a bit and turning her real comebacks into sharper retorts. Then she moves on to the pullover and weaves a story that could hardly have taken place in the minute or so before Gail got out of the car; but that's the only part she tells, as if Gail had stayed in the Tempo the whole time. It hardly matters by this point, though, because Gail is almost drifting off to sleep sitting up.

"Let me see that thing."

Gail tries to wave her off, but Cille insists, so she hands it to her. Cille paces up and down the room, looking for the spot with the most light and muttering about how ugly it is. She runs her fingertips over its surface.

"Who'd of thought you, of all people?" she laughs.

Gail smiles.

"Shoplifting!"

Cille is talking loudly enough to be heard outside of the room, and Gail motions her to keep her voice down.

"Ain't no point being shy about it now!"

"Cille, would you shut up!"

"Don't be shushing me—"

"I just don't want—"

Cille opens the door and waves the thing around in the night air. "Look, y'all!"

Gail jumps off the bed and grabs the figure from Cille, who stays where she is, in the open doorway, laughing. Gail stuffs it into a sock and pushes it deep among the clothes in her overnight bag.

"Now can we please go to bed?" Gail asks. "I'm really beat."

The peculiar calm from the roadside has worn off, and she closes her eyes to steady herself. All she meant was for her and Cille to have a laugh over the thing and the jerk from the store, just to have a good joke on the guy who treated Cille like crap, nothing more. The way Cille is acting now, though, she's beginning to wish she'd never touched the little figure.

"Go to bed? Gail, it's only ten-thirty. Let's go out, have a look around."

Gail stares at her. "Cille, are you out of your mind?"

"What's the big deal? It ain't late. Damn, you can wear your little jammies if that makes you feel better."

Gail opens her mouth, but nothing comes out. She just sits, dumbfounded by the turn of events in the space of a few minutes. Cille snatches up her keys, her purse, and her shoes, which she slips on with one hand. Despite the snuffling of the tired air conditioner, the air in the room seems quiet all around the churning center of her rushed actions.

"You coming?"

Gail looks at her.

"I said, are you coming? No, I didn't think so."

SOUVENIR

She slams the door behind her.

For hours, Gail sleeps soundly, and in her sleep she dreams of Melbourne. It isn't really Melbourne, of course, since she's never been that far down the coast, only to Daytona, with its sleazy bars and tacky little trinket booths right there on the beach. In her dreams everything cheap and seamy about Daytona disappears, and all that is left are palm trees and a brilliant swath of pure white sand that gives way to calm ocean water.

When she awakens in the empty room at three in the morning, she wonders why she wanted to come down here in the first place. She can't stand the Disney stuff, not any of it, the fake castles and princess crap that little white girls get into, the idiotic characters. Even as a child she was disgusted by it. She hates hot weather. When she was a kid, even the summers in Peekskill used to give her heat rash, and the corn silk her mother dusted her with did nothing but make her look like a fool. She rolls over in bed, which is still made up on Cille's side, but the question reverberates through her head so loudly she cannot fall back to sleep despite her exhaustion.

A week down here, plus her half of the car rental and the gas and tolls, is going to cost her at least five hundred, probably more if Cille gets her way. And for what, really, that's worth so much? Cille was right, Daytona was a waste of time, but would the next beach town down the coastline be any better? Would it let them get away from the Pop Connorses and Shells and trinket shops and cheap motels? They should have sought out something more than the tourist crap. They should have gone down to the Everglades. Cille never would have agreed to that, though, would have made fun of the idea. Gail can hear it without even trying: *Last thing we need is to be crawling around in some swamp full of alligators and mud and slime and shit, and it's full of snakes and damn, Gail, what the hell you want to go someplace like that for, anyway? Ain't nothing to do there but paddle around and you'd probably just wind up falling in and drowning and I'd have to drag your ass back to Peekskill and explain to your mother how it all happened.* As if this were any better. Gail rolls over and tries to go back to sleep.

They could still do it: just head for the ocean, follow the coastline, and not look back. Keep driving.

She rolls onto her back and looks at the ceiling. The traffic outside has dropped off to an occasional car whose headlights play briefly across a corner of the room before blinking away. She's known Cille for two years now, and still Cille keeps fooling her, keeps not being the car that throws its headlights through the window. She has to come back, though. Where else is she going to go? Surely she will eventually jiggle the lock and slip into the room, probably close to the time the sun is coming up, and give Gail a shake, and say it is time they got moving.

Maybe Gail will say no, she wants to sleep. Maybe she'll be dressed already, sitting there waiting, coolly smoking a cigarette. Maybe she won't even bother to ask where the hell Cille has been all night and sit there hanging on every word of the answer. Maybe she's had enough of that.

She drifts back to sleep replaying these possibilities in her head.

Later, the tinkling of metal awakens her.

There's something alarming in the noise; it's too deliberate to blend into the usual nighttime sounds of dripping water and creaking walls. Gail crawls out of bed and goes to the window, pushes the drapes back a little, and peers out.

Faint ocher smudges of approaching dawn hang in the sky. The Tempo is back in the lot, sitting out near the road under the Cameron's Motel sign. Two lights on the signpost shine down into the open engine compartment exposed by the car's raised hood. On the ground around the front of the car are strewn sections of hose, pipes, and lumps of disconnected engine parts that look as dead as eviscerated organs. Mixed in among them lie a couple of overturned plastic jugs and what might be tools. Cille stands off to the side a bit, one hand on her hip, the other punctuating her speech, watching the proceedings as a second figure, half in shadow, finishes up the job of disabling her and Cille's sole means of escape from this place.

There's a *clang* as he throws something metal onto the debris on the ground.

Gail lets the drape fall shut, rests her forehead against the textured cloth and the hard pane behind it, and stares at the floor. She's seen enough to know the rest, and know it with a kind of certainty that's new for her.

The details might vary, but of the gist Gail has no doubts. After Cille had trouble starting the car at a bar, or a nightclub, or maybe even Weber's parking lot, even there, he climbed out of his car and came over and helped get the Tempo running. Then he offered to follow her back to make sure she made it home safely along those dark, godforsaken roads. And once they got to Cameron's, he mentioned that he just happened to know a few things about cars and maybe he ought to take a look under the hood so there'd be no problems in the morning.

There is something about him. He lives nearby but he grew up in Jamaica, Queens, or Park Slope, Brooklyn, or maybe someplace close to New York City, like New Rochelle. Or he's from here and he looks it, but he narrows his eyes and calls the locals dimwit crackers the minute they're out of earshot. Or he seems to be from nowhere, from off the common map of speech and custom, and Cille is intrigued by his lack of interest in this town they are both just passing through and its people.

And now, he's letting on, he's sorry about the mess but he could give them a lift to a garage or to the nearest Hertz, an hour's drive from here, or, hell, it's been a while since he's seen Melbourne anyway. Why waste the rest of their vacation stranded with a cranky rental car that will take a week and cost a fortune to repair? Why not let Hertz deal with it? There's a *bang* when he lets the hood drop shut, and then the crunch of gravel as Cille approaches to tell Gail the whole suspicious story.

The air conditioner has finally caught up with the heat. It was just a matter of time, apparently. Particles of frozen air collide with the skin of Gail's naked arms and legs, chilling her down to the bone. She unzips her overnight bag to pull out clean clothes for the day, but deep among the T-shirts and underwear her hand finds the sock with the bulge in it, and she stops. It's still warm. Has it somehow held the heat of the day before? She'd like to get rid of it, but it's hers now. Out on the road, Cille will tell him about the whole Weber's incident in the spreading light that finally reveals the look of the place where they've spent the night. "Get it out, Gail, let him see the damn thing," Cille will say.

An untended, reeling sign planted at the side of the road will announce, as they cross the town line, the name of the place they are leaving. Green Springs, or Foglerville, or Yemahassee. But Gail already knows where they've been. Leaving town, with the Tempo behind them and the open road ahead, she will be holding onto the possibility that she does not know just as well where they are going.

MARISOL'S THINGS

Years later, I thought I remembered that day with perfect clarity.

First came the storm so wild we just knew it would knock out the power. It didn't. Still we had hopes of an upended tree or two, or at least some downed wires, and as soon as the rain ended, my sister Marisol and I ran outside.

We were six and ten then, and already a baffling reversal had set in, for it was I, the older, who had trouble keeping up with Marisol at times like this. She streaked ahead into the back yard, where leaves lay scattered over the lawn, their whitish undersides turned up. Trash can lids were piled against the chain-link fence at the back of our lot. But that was it, the sum of the damage. Hardly the disaster we'd hoped for.

It wasn't the first storm we'd seen. It was hardly our first romp through the yard after some blast of rough weather. But it was one of those days, I came to believe, that might have gone differently; when I might have said or done a thing I didn't say or do and sent the cascade of years down a different path than the one it would take.

The storm had left Mrs. Fast's ancient oak tree standing. Marisol and I meandered toward it through the wet grass, silent in our disappointment. But there, at the base of the tree, we found something. It took us a moment to identify it, it was so battered. A sock, I thought, or a squished cap.

"It's a squirrel," Marisol said.

He lay at the base of the tree, at the bottom of a raw, yellow gash in the bark that ran all the way up into the lowermost limbs. Just looking, we could hear the sounds of his death all too vividly: the sudden crack of lightning, the wind tearing through the branches, the rasping of claws trying to stop the plunge to the ground. Marisol stepped back.

"Let's go home," she said.

Thumb in her mouth, hovering a few steps behind me, she looked even more the baby than usual. The halo of fine, raisin-brown hair that always pulled loose from her braids floated around her head. Heat rash prickled the auburn skin of her thin arms.

"Go on, chicken," I said. "Just miss everything."

I wanted to poke at the thing, roll it over, examine it, and I wanted Marisol to watch. I was sure that was what she needed. Sometimes she seemed such a raw child, still too wet for the world. The problem was, I believed that God had struck the squirrel dead with a bolt of lightning. What else could have made that gash? So how could I dare to touch him?

"Will the other squirrels come and bury him?" my sister asked.

She had crept forward again and was back beside me.

"Of course not," I said. I thought about it. "Well, I don't think so."

She slipped past me before I could grab her. Down on her knees in the grass, she folded the squirrel up in her skirt, and then she headed off toward our own yard without waiting for me. I collected myself and followed her. In the back, near the fence, she dug a shallow hole, slid the squirrel in, covered him, and patted down the dirt. I waited for her to say a prayer, or some Marisol-like contortion of one (Our Father, who art in heaven, Hollywood be thy name . . .) over her handiwork.

"So now," she said, "he can rise up to heaven."

She stood up and wiped her filthy hands down the front of her yellow jumper. I was still back at the tree, in my mind, still unable to even finger the yellow gash, and it must have showed on my face. Catching me staring at her, Marisol turned her gaze back to the burial mound.

"Or he can stay underground if he wants to," she said. "Right?"

⌒

Later, after we'd gone to bed, we talked in the dark until my mother called upstairs and reminded us that tomorrow was a school day. As we lay waiting for sleep, I asked Marisol if she'd washed her hands.

She hesitated a moment.

"I think so," she said.

"Because there's diseases you can catch," I said. "Carried by germs too small for you to see. They can get in your blood. You have to be careful."

For a moment she lay quietly. Then she slid from under the covers and went out in the hall. Though she closed the bathroom door, I listened until I heard the faint whir of water from the tap. I pictured her small hands under the stream, rubbing the soap, missing only the tiny crevices where finger met palm and nail met fingertip.

Marisol broke bones. At seven, it was her wrist. At ten, a hairline fracture of something the doctor called her coronoid process. They didn't set that one because it's in your face, under your cheek, and what could they do, put a cast around her head? This situation worried me, and whenever I could I would sit with my sister, who'd been instructed not to run, jump, or crawl around, even talk or laugh more than was absolutely necessary. I thought it a mistake not to set the fracture. A cast would have been a burden, especially in July, but not so awful as a bone that fused itself wrong, in a lump or at an angle. A scar hiding under her skin.

So I watched Marisol for any sign that a problem might be developing and pretty soon her endangered face haunted me at the roller-skating rink, in the dusty stacks of the city library, even at night in my dreams. I needed only to let my thoughts drift for a moment and there she was, the huge brown near-lashless eyes, the frizz of hair so soft it never even tangled when my mother combed it, the pointed chin on her round face, the premature hunch of her bony shoulders. We sat with the television off, not talking. Cicadas hummed and R&B ballads from transistor radios drifted in on the occasional breeze.

The family skipped its usual summer vacation that year, two

weeks in Misquamicut, Rhode Island, floating in the frigid ocean among the jellyfish that gathered like a naval blockade along the shoreline. Keeping an eye on Marisol was my summer project. And just as firmly as images of other summer trips were arrested on film for our scrapbooks, Marisol entered my mind as she was then, a child of perfect stillness.

Marisol's coronoid process healed. But my weeks of scrutiny had tipped a balance, and when I looked around I found myself no longer shadowed. Marisol stopped trailing me to the corner store, ceased bugging me to play jacks with her. In my new and unsought freedom I felt larger, older, even expansive now and then. I blew whole days at the mall with my two best friends, joined the track team, developed an interest in older boys. Still I tried to get a rundown on my sister's day each night, before we went to sleep.

Marisol continued to break things. One morning I heard the crash of a plate shattering in the kitchen and the raised voice of my mother. And then Marisol, screaming in reply. A few months later, she broke the glass of the front-door window late at night. How? From the back and forth between Marisol and my father, I could make no sense of it. I still had the motionless child in mind, could not connect her to the angry sister my mother wrapped in a towel and drove to the hospital emergency room, full of cuts and shards.

I asked her what had happened. An accident, she said. I broke the glass by accident.

One morning as we were dressing for school, I watched her put on pantyhose, cobalt blue with a hint of iridescence. How, I wondered, did a twelve-year-old know where to buy such things? She slipped them out of a clear plastic package and placed one gathered side over her left big toe. Slowly, with her fingertips, she covered the other toes and drew the shimmering weave up her calf, over her knee, up her thigh. She repeated the moves with her right leg. Five minutes passed before I reached the startled conclusion that she was enjoying herself.

Then she sat on the edge of the bed, looking at her legs. In spite of myself, my wish to focus on the moment and make sense of it,

Marisol's Things

I thought of her in other clothes. The outfit she made for her first day of kindergarten, which puzzled us all, a black bodice with delicate red tissue paper bunched and stapled at the hem, the arm-holes, and coming up from the neck to hide half her face. The scraggly "Indian" headdress, a lumpy paper band embedded with dyed feathers that she'd begged for and worn for days on a family trip years before to Niagara Falls. Costumes, I thought, then and now; costumes, the blue pantyhose, too, and maybe even the yellow jumper, disguising the girl inside them.

"Marisol?" I said.

She looked up. But I didn't say more. I wasn't sure what to ask.

My eighteenth year, shortly before I was to leave for college, it turned prematurely cool. Our city's mid-August bicentennial celebration was wrapping up its final weekend in Worrall Park, a riverfront strip reclaimed from factory ruins and the rubble-strewn field that once surrounded them. Food booths and stilt-walkers were promised by the newspaper, with fireworks at dusk. I could find nobody to walk down with.

"Why don't you take your sister?" my father said over the folded edge of the *Winnikee Falls Journal*. "You act like you're not related."

The thought of taking her had not occurred to me, but I protested anyway. "I do not."

"When's the last time you took her with you?"

"She doesn't want to go."

"How would you know?"

How could I not know? He knew how weird she was. She wandered around like a vagrant all day. Don't go too far, my mother would tell her, and away she went, running one hand along her thin single braid over and over, her gangly figure loping down to the corner, across the street, right out of sight. My parents took to buying her thick, heavy shoes because she wore through the soles of regular sneakers and sandals. The day would pass; I might glimpse her at the edge of a field or coming out of a store on Main Street. Then at dinner, there she would be, dusty and tired, with Ritz cracker crumbs in her clothes.

Only at night did she stay indoors. After a hasty wash in the bathroom sink, and the discarding of her knapsack with its few remaining Ritz crackers, she fell into a coma sleep the minute she hit the bed. We'd ended our after-dark chats.

But my father's words had stung me, and I went through the motions of asking her. Marisol surprised me by accepting.

For a while we wandered around among the historical dioramas and the mosaic of the colonial flag made by a local elementary school. She stayed a step behind me all the while and said little more than "Look at this," or "Look at that." I asked if she wanted ice cream, cotton candy, hot dogs, anything, whatever she wanted. I had a summer job at the IGA, bagging groceries and corralling carts, and craved the chance to buy things for her. Finally she relented and had a knish. Then a candy apple and a bag of caramel popcorn. Then she asked for a piece of blueberry pie from a stand run by the Daughters of the American Revolution, two of whom sat pink and sweating in frowsy eighteenth-century dresses and caps behind their table.

We got into line behind an old couple who couldn't make up their minds and were debating the merits of the various pies and cookies spread in front of them. Finally we reached the table and one of the Daughters handed me two slices of pie that oozed glistening purple filling. Marisol and I walked several paces away from the stand. The sun bounced heat waves off the concrete walks and plastic tents. I chewed my pie deliberately. Fork in hand, Marisol rubbed her eyes for a moment. She backed into the shade of a tent and ate her entire slice.

"Do you want to go home now?" I asked.

We'd been there all of forty-five minutes. Marisol nodded.

And for a while she was that child again, impossibly still, holding herself a certain way even as she walked, and walking at a pace so regular she could have been measuring her steps. We made it half the way home. Then she threw it up, all of it, on the sidewalk, on a fire hydrant, her shins and socks, and her scuffed lace-ups, but most of it, including the blueberries, on me. I didn't get angry. I knew I deserved it. I took us into a Trailways station and, in the dirty bathroom, we cleaned up as best we could.

During my last year of college, I made a rare trip home for the wedding of a cousin. I took a taxi from the train station straight to the church. Marisol hadn't arrived when the ceremony started. She came in late, thought about threading over to where our parents and I sat in the middle of a row, and then slipped into a pew in the back. In her white, high-collared, long-sleeved Laura Ashley dress with a ruffled skirt and cuffs, she looked more like a casual bride than a serious guest. I remembered the blue pantyhose and imagined them under the white dress, and I thought I would have to suppress snorts of laughter. But none came.

After the ceremony I thought about trying to find her but decided not to. She wouldn't stay long, and I had to rush off to catch the train back to New York City. I kissed my parents good-bye, waved at the newlyweds, then slid through the buzzing crowd to the door. Marisol stood just outside on the steps, holding a lighter to a cigarette dangling off her lower lip. Before I knew what I was doing, I snatched the cigarette and smashed it under my heel.

"Oh my God, I'm sorry. I'm so sorry," I said.

"S'awright," she replied.

She lit another and puffed deeply, then she offered me the package. I took one, and she lit it for me. It was an unfamiliar brand, and tasted vaguely of celery.

"Hypocrite," she said.

I laughed, and she smiled through the screen of smoke we'd set up. She'd relaxed her hair and waved it straight back from her forehead, a mistake given its softness, for the sun shone right through it in places. Then I recognized the style. It was the same as my mother's. So was the shade on her lips.

"Do me a favor," she said. "I need to get away for a little while. Three or four weeks."

"Away?" I asked. "Where? What about school?"

She had the rest of her senior year of high school to finish; it was only October. And she was a good student. My mother told me, when I called home, about the A average Marisol was keeping up.

In answer, she just waved. "Kind of an experience I can't miss."

She dropped the cigarette, cursed, and picked it up again. She brushed off the end of it and put it back in her mouth, but coughed when she tried to inhale. From that point on we looked at the steps or the cars passing on the street, and I gave up casting around for a way to dissuade her.

"Tell them for me."

"What?"

"Tell them something. Explain it to them."

I knew why she asked. They didn't worry about me, my parents. Whatever else they thought of me—and this was a subject I didn't wish to probe too deeply—whatever else, they knew I would not wind up in an overturned car, or with a brutal man, or harboring a medicine cabinet full of pills. They would not open the *Winnikee Falls Journal* and find a four-line item about me on a back page. Marisol wanted to console them with a little of this trust.

She backed down the stairs without telling me anything more. She didn't even say she would explain later. In a moment she was kicking through the tumble of autumn leaves rolling down the wide sidewalk of Carter Boulevard, and finally, years too late, I let go of the motionless little girl of my memory and replaced her with this Marisol: a white dress, a few oblique words, an unspoken promise shrewdly collected on, and a slow fade into the sun.

All I wanted for a long time was no alarm clock in the morning, a nice tray of Stouffer's macaroni and cheese out of the microwave for late breakfast, and snow. Not the pristine, white stuff forming soft blankets on the sloping roofs of churches and little hats on fire hydrants. No. I waited for the melt and freeze, the pounding of car tires, the eruption of dirt from underneath that turned the snow into muck scumming up windshields and caking the edges of sewer grates. The streets gone foul with slush; that was what I craved.

Albany obliged. I had ended my marriage after only a year on a principle which afterward struck me as so absurd that I could hardly believe my own actions. Thomas had loved me too passionately. His lovemaking had been like absorption, his kisses the mouth of a vortex. I feared I might vanish. I thought to reestablish myself by getting away from him. But I had long since forgotten why I was bothering with graduate school, and in little time the history department was sending me threatening letters about finishing my thesis or withdrawing for good.

My roommate, Chrissie, knocked on my door promptly at eight each morning in a futile effort to coax me out of my bedroom. Inside, I lay around looking out the window at the slush in the parking lot below and waiting for new snow to gather in the clouds on the western horizon.

Going home and starting over, it seemed, was the thing to do. But I was thirty, too long flown from my parents' nest, too loaded down with the debris of bad choices and missed chances. And besides, Marisol still lived in Winnikoo Falls, and I could not imagine what we'd do with one another. My sister and I had not spoken in a couple of years, but my mother called me now and then and kept me up to date on family news. I knew Marisol was in a training program for teachers' aides, that her marriage to a fellow from our hometown named Roderick was floundering, that part of the problem was her inability to get pregnant.

When my mother phoned on a Friday night and told me about her bingo winnings and my father's golf game, I hardly listened to her. It had begun to snow in Albany, and I wanted to go watch.

"Wait a minute," she said after a while, sensing, probably, that my mind was elsewhere. "Marisol's here. Let me put your sister on."

Before I could object, the line went quiet. I cast around in my mind for fragments of the last conversation we'd had, but my thoughts went blank.

The line clicked and scraped, and Marisol spoke.

"You coming home for Christmas?" she asked.

"Uh, uh," I stammered, caught off guard; that was the last thing I planned to do. "I don't know, I have a lot of work to turn in—"

Marisol laughed a husky laugh, and I thought of the cigarettes at the church. "It's no big deal," she said. "I just thought it'd be fun, you know. To reminisce about when we were kids."

She sounded as if all the years that had welled up between us had never happened, as if she wanted to revel in some TV-show childhood she'd made up in her imagination. I didn't know what to say.

"Sorry about Thomas," she said.

"Thomas?" I'd never even introduced her to my ex-husband. "Oh. Thomas. Thank you."

A few moments passed.

I said, "And I'm sorry about, you know, about—"

"Yeah, that. Well, them's the breaks, eh?"

More silence.

"Well," said Marisol, heaving a sigh that signaled an end to the conversation, "you think about it. Okay?"

Before I could summon another excuse, the line went quiet again. I heard some voices in the background, then my mother came on and told me good-bye in the roundabout way she had.

That evening, I dug around in my bureau until I found the Amtrak schedule I kept there. I left it on top, tucked under the edge of the mirror, for the next two weeks. In that time I got Chrissie to leave me alone in the morning by telling her I was going to visit my family for Christmas. She left three days before the holiday. Instead of packing a suitcase, I lay down and slept through the holiday sales, the Salvation Army drive, the carolers, the seasonal TV specials, including the Grinch, and the free mulled cider in the dorm lobby. If I could have, I would have slept until spring.

A few years later, my parents lost their house in an eminent domain dispute. The city of Winnikee Falls wanted to widen a busy street and notified the owners of ten or twelve houses along the route that they would have to move. The homeowners formed an organization to fight the city, but I could tell from the way my mother chatted blithely about their activities that my parents were making only a halfhearted effort. The fight lasted about six months.

I flew in from Chicago and took a bus from New York City to Winnikee Falls. New York was into the balmy heart of spring, but Winnikee Falls, farther up the Hudson River, was still chilly. When I arrived, the house was full of boxes. My parents had bought a smaller house in the suburbs and did not seem the least bit perturbed about selling the family homestead.

"Most of your stuff's up in the attic," my mother told me. "We didn't touch it. Left it all for you. But anything you don't take goes out with the trash."

She bustled off in a pair of beat-up jeans and a T-shirt. I stood there with a lump in my throat. Didn't she want to keep my kindergarten report cards? My papier-mâché toad from third grade? My father breezed by with a box of books to donate to the library. I stopped myself from stopping him. If they had decided it was time to sweep away the past, so be it. I found some green trash bags in the kitchen and trudged upstairs to the attic.

The main attic room, the big one, was a messy time capsule from the seventies. I dove in and snatched up polyester shirts, Jackson Five posters, platform shoes, bent picks, Barbie dolls, eight-track tapes. I wasn't sure whether some of it had belonged to me or to Marisol. Into the green bags went all of it. I had decided at the start that I had better get done and get out of there fast, because I didn't want to throw away one bit of it. It was nothing more than a desiccated museum, really, the scattered cargo of a ship that should have sailed long ago. But I was not ready. Thirty-four years old, and here I was lingering and clinging, like a child wheedling for a little more time before bed.

After an hour I stopped and dragged three bags of stuff downstairs and out to the curb. My dad was there smoking a cigarette.

"Good," he said. "You can give us a hand with those." He pointed to the front porch, where he had stacked at least ten good-sized, bulging cardboard boxes.

"What's all that?" I asked.

"Marisol's things," he said, and tossed his glowing butt into the street.

She drove up in a hatchback in the middle of his story about the three days she had spent combing through every room of the attic, filling those boxes. After she climbed out through the passenger door, she gave my father a kiss and me a hug.

"Guess you couldn't fly all this back to Chicago," she said, looking at the bags I'd dumped on the curb.

I shrugged lamely. I wanted to hide them, every embarrassing one of them, from her careful collector's eye. I hardly said a word as the three of us piled boxes into the back of her little white hatchback with its dented driver's-side door. As I was hauling out to the car one of the last boxes we would be able to fit, I tripped over a green bag and it fell open, spilling some of its contents onto the sidewalk. My father had gone back in the house by then.

"Shit," I said, and turned my back on it and walked out into the middle of the dark and empty street.

She went over and began putting things back in the bag.

"Don't," I said. "Just leave it."

But she ignored me and finished. She even found the bread tie and wound the top of the bag shut. Then she walked out in the street to where I was standing.

We were far enough away from the streetlights that it was dark where we stood, and I couldn't see Marisol very well. Her shadowy form seemed unfamiliar, metamorphosed from the young woman in the white dress at my cousin's wedding into someone I, once again, didn't quite know.

"You remember that dead squirrel we found after that storm?" she said.

"What squirrel?" I said.

"In Mrs. Fast's yard? When I was five or six, I think?"

Then it came trickling back to me. The gash. Her yellow jumper. I nodded.

"And I buried him? You remember you said not to touch him because he had a curse on him?"

I groaned. "My God. I don't remember that. Did I really *say* that to you?"

"Oh yeah," Marisol said. And she laughed. "Cursed. But I didn't believe you."

"What?"

"Didn't believe a word of it."

"You didn't?"

"Nope."

"Thank God," I said.

"Thank God? Thank God? Look, it wouldn't have been a national disaster even if I had, okay? You blow things out of proportion. You make everything a crisis."

She lit a cigarette and offered me one.

"You're just like Roderick. He used to do the same thing. Drove me nuts. The baby thing, he just couldn't let it ride for a while, and that's why we split up before we knew Syl was coming. It was so stupid."

The chilly air had developed enough of a bite that I felt the tug of the warm attic, the pull of its shelter calling me back.

"So why didn't you get back together after she was born?" I asked.

Marisol took a long time before she answered.

"It was too late by then. Just too late." She didn't elaborate.

The headlights of a car flashed at us as it turned onto our block.

"Let's get out of the middle of the street," she said.

At the curb, her car sagged alarmingly under the weight of all those boxes. They filled the rear compartment, the passenger seat, even the floor up front. She opened the door, took a box off the passenger seat, and sat it on the curb.

"Come over and meet your niece," she said.

I nudged the box with the toe of my shoe.

"She's, what, two now?"

"Three and a half. Take this."

We stacked boxes next to the bags. When we'd cleared a space, Marisol climbed in through the passenger side to get to the driver's seat. I sat next to her. My seat sagged to one side, and the musty scent of the upholstery and carpeting almost overwhelmed me when I shut the door. She started the engine and worked the clutch and gears until the car jerked out into the street and then rolled along more smoothly. I had never been driven by Marisol before. She cruised along the dark streets a little too fast for my taste. She lit another cigarette, rolled her window down partway, and flicked ash out into the breeze. I looked around to make sure she hadn't set the boxes in the back on fire, and after a while decided not to watch how close she got before she stopped behind other cars at lights.

"You comfortable?" she asked.

"Sure," I said.

She laughed at me. "Liar."

"Good God, Marisol. Who the hell taught you how to drive?" I finally asked her. "Mario Andretti?"

"Who taught me? Huh!" she said, and sat up a little straighter. "I taught myself."

Keep Looking

A stranger is watching you in a bookstore.

Here you are, looking for a little peace after a hellish day at work, only to find some man staring at you as if it is his God-given right. You could stare right back. That's probably what one of those women's self-defense manuals would tell you to do, to puff yourself up, look formidable, try not to appear the vulnerable type. But instead you settle for massaging your indignation and wondering just how long he has held you under the lens of his gaze.

You came in at least half an hour ago. Maybe more. And you spent most of that time right here in the World History section, sitting cross-legged on the floor in a way that was sure to ruin the linen slacks you wore to work. But you didn't care. You wanted to forget work, the spectacle of your fellow programmers scrambling for cover when the call came in from Mercy Hospital saying that its computer system had started churning up phantom patients whose ICD-9's indicated ailments enough to kill them and their families too. Half of your colleagues at Cayuga Systems had tried to look heroic at someone else's expense, and the rest had become wide-eyed in their innocence. Nine o'clock before you got out of there, away from those people.

Immersing yourself in a new paperback about the Gypsies of Europe had started to take your mind off the place. The twitch in your eyebrow ceased. You read two of the chapters in their entirety and not even you, if you were to be honest, would call that browsing, but you were well into another chapter, you were fingering the edge of a page you were about to turn, anticipating the hollow-eyed, clustered faces in the black-and-white photographs, when you felt it. You looked up. There was nothing amiss, nothing apparent to the eye, but people say it happens like that. You just catch a vibe. You've heard how it works: *Most folks got it, at least a bit of that sense, but some folks, well, they forget where they come from and that's that. They're out of touch. Might as well be blind.* You're never sure which camp you're in, and it's one more thing you prefer not to think about, so back into the story of the Gypsies you plunged, all concentration. But when your hand reached again for the edge of the page, your eyes traveled up from the book, and you saw a man staring at you.

Your heart surged; you turned the page. You searched the faces of the family there, a ragtag group with a slew of children posed around a rickety, horse-drawn cart. Armenia, 1924. So many children scattered among the adults, shared among them like food until the relations of mother to son, uncle to niece, blurred into the bond of the tribe. But relations between you and the Gypsies felt disconcertingly out of kilter for a second, as if you had somehow forgotten the names that were not given in the lackadaisical caption, names you once knew. Surely if you strained a little, stretched the memory, you could bring them back to you from the oblivion of the forgotten. But that was impossible, of course. You knew neither the Gypsies, nor the browsers around you, nor the consumptively thin, tar-complexioned man with black hair spiking from under a hat who was staring at you.

Yes, you saw that much of him.

Knowing you are watched sends an odd tingling rush over your skin. At least you hadn't changed into your jeans, the ones full of holes you've stubbornly kept wearing as your body filled out to a postcollegiate womanliness, straining the double-stitched seams. What did David say about them when he kicked them out of the bathroom doorway the other morning? Rags. Indecent in daylight. *You don't live in a dorm anymore, Lisa, those years are over and gone, so toss the damned jeans and that ratty Spelman T-shirt too; I'm sick of looking at them.* He cursed his razor, threw it in the sink, and pulled on his tie, muttering something about letting them fire him if they couldn't deal with a little beard.

Now, you catch yourself running your hand along the inside seam of your linen slacks, drawn as hard and tight across your thigh as an anchoring rope, and stop abruptly, realizing they're no better than the jeans. They cover nothing, protect nothing. This man has seen you, seen the dark tangle and wave of your hair and the distinctive fade at your temples, the thinness you try to hide. He has seen the way your scarf bunches because you've tied it too tightly at your throat. He's noted the way your hands move about when you've forgotten them, touching, checking, making sure that no part of yourself has betrayed a stray thought in your head. But is that not in itself a sign language?

You drop the book, curse your clumsiness, and pick it up as you begin a banal recitation: This is Zack's Books and Curios, it is located on Preston Street, you have been here a hundred times, maybe a thousand. Or more. In the back north corner, there is an old grate in the floor where you can look down into the basement below. Eleven o'clock is closing time. People say that Wacker, Zack's dog, bit off the tip of Zack's little finger and that is why he never fully opens the fist of his right hand. The single brick step out front, the pink couch in the window, the shelf of books on mermaids, fat old Zack with his greasy hair and suspenders. The cowbell over the door. The sign on the register: *Legal tender only.* You've got it all right, completely right, you know exactly how it is, and yet when you look up again the man in the hat is staring right at you.

You get up so quickly that your legs, numb from contortion, nearly give out under you. You shove the book on Gypsies back among the ones on the shelf and move in a palsied stumble toward Science and Technology. There, in the corner, you plant yourself and turn, intending to face him: some raggedy-assed junkie fool you wouldn't give the time of day if he bothered you anywhere else. Hell. Some sorry retard who missed the bus back to the group home. You put your hands on your hips and your chin in the air, and you wait for him. But oddly enough, he doesn't show, and pretty soon you relax your rigid posture, which is impossible to hold for long, for you anyway, and not long after that, keeping an eye out for the man, you pull a new volume off the shelf.

You flip through it—a picture book about Sikorsky and the helicopter. Photos of early, failed predecessors, big clumsy things with bizarrely huge or tiny rotors tacked to strange spots on the body. Then Sikorsky's prototypes, and finally the first model to stay aloft, its blades a blur of light and air that seems like a granted wish on the wind. In junior high school you made something like it: a cloud in a bottle. You scrounged a bike pump, bought rubbing alcohol, stole your mother's favorite glass vase, rigged a plug with a piece of cork and modeling clay and even some bubble gum around the hose where it pierced the cork. On the appointed day you carted the contraption to the front of the class and set it up on a table. With no gauge to guide you, you pumped up the pressure, waited for the right moment, and then released. And there it was, for a fraction of a second floating right in the vase, an ethereal wisp, an angel summoned by your book smarts and a stirring in your chest that had told you, at just the right moment, *Now, let go now.* You looked up at your science class, expectant. *I don't see nothin'*, someone said, and then there were giggles, laughter. But you saw it, that once, even if you never have managed to conjure a cloud again.

You reach to put the book back and your eyes scan the room and you realize that one of the heads visible over the tops of the shelves near Fiction belongs to the man who was watching you. With his back turned, and the hat removed from his head of black hair flattened as if by a vise, you had missed him. You shake your head absurdly, as if it would stop the fluttering of your mind from man to book to floor to white rectangle of index card tacked to a shelf inches from your shoulder. *IF YOU CAN'T FIND IT,* the card says, *keep looking!*

"*Fuck* this," you spit.

He turns and looks at you with round black eyes.

You march toward the door. First straight down an aisle, then zigzag around an offset shelf and halfway down the next aisle. A gray-haired man in glasses and beret blocks your progress. You mutter a loud *Excuse me,* but he remains in place as if you've not said a word. You repeat it louder, and this time he takes his hand from his pocket and fingers the head of a wooden cane. You see, now, the cast on his foot and the way he is wedged against the shelf behind him for support. And beyond him you see the street through the dingy front window, its pavement awash in yellow from the lamp above.

You expect that he will block your route, that his black form will drift across the way like a car from a side road pulling into your path at night, too late for your brakes. But he does not. You make it to the end of the aisle without sighting him, pass through the tall shelves housing Psychology, Architecture, Current Events, alone. Your pace falters and your legs fail you just as you come within sight of the counter. You turn and scan a wide circle. He does not let you see him.

But you know he can see you. Can't he? You know that he can, you can feel it, the feeling primordial, so deep within you it seems almost to slip away the instant you notice it. Almost. What was it your father used to do? Into his study he went after work every night, the claustrophobic little room converted from a pantry, and tallied figures on that big desktop adding machine of his until your mother tapped lightly on the door and announced dinner. He was punching in numbers, running them through calculations. The snap and whir of that lever was the pulse of the entire house. At thirteen you decided that he was not, could not be, must not be, related to you by blood.

"Help you?" asks the boy at the front counter.

You've drifted without knowing it.

"No," you say. Then, "Yes."

Both of you wait. Then you stab with a finger at sticks of incense under the glass. You buy three sticks, and the bag he gives you is good, you realize as you walk away, good for the way it lets you clench something.

You are nearly out the door before you see him. In the window, under the arch formed by the painted words *soiruC dna skooB*, his reflection leaps into view as you reach the place where the angle is right. On the tattered pink couch facing Preston Street, he is slouched down low enough to make his head invisible over the high back. He's heard the clumsy exchange at the counter. He knows you hesitated there, you are sure of it. So far he's gotten everything he wanted from you. He's not a fool, not a retard either, and you wonder why you thought him those things, what those words mean, even

If you leave now, without meeting his stare, he will be a joke to tell David over breakfast tomorrow morning. *You wouldn't believe! Right there in Zack's. I'm serious!* Or maybe you won't mention him to David at all, at least not while David is on edge about not getting the promotion, not while he's testing the idea of filing a bias suit with every sip of black coffee he rolls over his tongue. Maybe you won't even mention it to yourself after tonight. You push through the door with your eyes straight ahead, and you keep going even when the cowbell startles you. Then you are outside, misted by a light rain and cooled by the October night. In another moment you are past the window of Zack's without a backward glance. If you move quickly, you will be safely away, and in a few moments you reach your car, parked just around the corner on a side street, and get in.

But the convertible top thumps and moans when you try to raise it, refusing to go up. The rain pelts you a little harder. You toss the bag of incense on the dash. The seats, the stick shift, and the steering wheel are all slick with moisture. It's a restored Austin-Healey convertible, a car David calls a waste-of-money toy, a gift from your parents for your high school graduation. You've not forgotten that afternoon. Spackenkill High, 1990. Commencement day, your teens nearing an end. Miss Thomas took you aside in the hall and reminded you to be proud of your heritage when you went out into the world; as if she didn't know you were headed for Spelman, that safe harbor. Her purplish lips pressed firm enough for a kiss, the hand on her bangled wrist caressing your shoulders like one would rub a colicky baby's. And then Mr. Cowper, not a half hour later, cornered you down by the teachers' lounge and bent so close you could smell the Dixie Peach in his hair. *Crabs in a basket, that's what we are,* he said, gripping your arm so tightly it brought tears to your eyes. *You get up near the top, like you might get out, and they pull you back down with the rest.* When he was sure you'd heard him, he let go, and you ran down the hall, high heels clicking, black gown flapping, your mortarboard lost somewhere behind you.

You sit for some time, lost in that day, before you go back to the corner and look down Preston Street. The sidewalk is empty, the man is not loping toward you. Impossible. Isn't it?

Confused, you start back toward Zack's, where there is a phone. David will complain about your calling him out on a night like this because of your stupid toy, but complaint has become his tuning note, his perfect C, and you understand it is not really directed at you. When you get near Zack's, it looks like the lights are out; from up close you see that they are. You don't believe it could be so late. But when you hold your watch up under one of the yellow street-lights, the hands read 11:02. In the quiet, you can almost hear the snap and whir of the mechanism spinning those hands. A car drives by, and its wheels seem to sizzle on the cool, wet pavement.

You walk along, looking for him. You examine doorways, the spaces under cars, the benches in the park diagonally across from Zack's. He is somewhere nearby, just out of sight. Isn't he? You walk another block, two, three, passing a public telephone from which you could call David for a ride. The only people on the streets are a middle-aged white man carrying a bag of groceries, who does not look up when you pass, and a woman who might be a little younger than you, Latina maybe, who flinches and clutches the collar of her sweater shut when you pass her. You ignore her and circle back toward Zack's, scouring the empty streets again. Your breath, fast and heavy, pummels your ears.

Unbidden, the Gypsies come back to you, and you swipe at the air to brush them away. In Zack's, you had flipped to the last chapter of the book. Warsaw, 1994. No pictures with that one. All those centuries of roaming and endurance come down to a few old people too frail to withstand the camera's gaze. And now, as you walk along the rain-slicked street, the night falls into a series of planes, cold, glassy surfaces with sharp, right-angled edges. The storefronts and brick walk-ups around you shimmer and distort. You don't bother closing your eyes. You've seen this before, hun-dreds of times, maybe a thousand. A dog urinating against a tree flickers as if he might wink away entirely. What is it, unseen, that binds all the planes together? It has evaded you again, just like that delicate cloud.

Keep Looking

You find your way back to the telephone and drop a quarter into the slot. The phone clicks, the dial tone resumes. You press your forehead against the molded plastic face of the receiver. You could call David. You could call your mother, your father, Ginny or Raquel, your best friends, Julia or Keisha from Delta Sigma Theta, the door-man who works nights at your office building, nice man, even Miss Thomas. Any of them, any voice, would do; just so long as you no longer have to listen to your own.

Passage

In Grand Central when you looked up you could see stars painted across the ceiling. Thelma Stewart remembered that, though she hadn't been inside of Grand Central for over forty years. It was hard to believe, but it had been just as long since she'd set foot in the station here in Winnikee Falls too, though she lived only a few blocks away. It had changed little over time, though the bricks in the high walls, once red, ocher, and brown, had dulled to a uniform blackish gray. The two-story windows still allowed in surprisingly little light, giving the waiting room a twilit gloom even in the middle of the day. Only after dark would it become bright, with the bulbs in the old chandeliers giving off a strange glare like a continuous camera flash.

Twice in the past week, and once in the week before that, she'd made her way through the muggy July heat, along the buckling sidewalks in the older part of town, to the train station. She'd sat there for hours on one of the long, polished wooden benches and at the end of it all, she recalled only the simplest bits of her thoughts. Her dead husband, Earl, striding across the floor toward her, waving a burly hand, a striped short-billed cap tucked under his arm, his nickel-gray overalls stenciled with grease and dirt from his day's work on the tracks. Or Earl, guiding her through the brushy woods at the station's north end to a spot where she sees the impossible thing he's promised: a fat, yellow moon balanced atop a spire of the Mid-Hudson Bridge. The rest was a blur. Hours gone in a blur, and she wondered how that could be. She was not the kind of person who let her mind wander off from her like some stray dog,

wallowing in puddles and nibbling on anything that passed under
its wet nose.

Across the cavernous waiting room, two men talked in a corner.
Thelma had seen them before, the shorter one pushing around a
dust mop, the taller one passing back and forth occasionally between
the doors to the tracks and the unmarked doors that led into the
recesses of the station. Now they seemed to have noticed her, and
the shorter one kept looking over at her. The last thing she wanted
was to be bothered by them, so she got up and went over to the
ticket window.

"What time's the next train to New York gonna be here?" she
asked the young Oriental woman behind the barred glass.

"Do you want the Metro North or the Amtrak?" the ticket seller
asked without raising her head from what she was reading.

"I don't care." She wasn't sure of the difference, and it didn't
matter.

"Well, I can't decide for you."

Thelma looked at the girl. "Metro North."

The girl punched the buttons of a machine, which whirred quietly for a moment. "That'll be $17.50," she said.

"Did I ask you for a ticket?" Thelma said.

The girl looked at her as if she did not understand what Thelma
meant.

"No, I didn't. What I asked you was, what time is the New York
train leaving? If you paid attention, you'd a heard me the first time
I said it."

All that got her was a schedule. She tucked the paper sprinkled
with tiny green lettering under her arm and walked away from the
window. What did she expect, snapping at people like that? She'd
been doing it a lot lately, even with her son, Alphonse, who was
only trying to help her. It surprised her to hear words like that come
tumbling out of her mouth.

The two men were still clustered in the far corner, talking and
glancing. At home, Alphonse had probably arrived, let himself in
with his key, and gotten back to work patching that crack in the
upstairs wall that he'd found a week ago. She spread the schedule
open and ran a quick glance over all the times and arrows and lines

and shaded areas, and then folded the useless thing up again. The thing with trains was, one always came eventually. You waited, but you waited inside a sure kind of knowledge that made time pass like a soothing hand on the back.

That train gang was the hardest work Earl ever did, he told her more than once in the years after he left it. But it was a regular job, and the pay was regular too, and she had agreed to marry him during the year that he worked on the railroad. In that year, he never missed a day. Thelma slid the schedule into her purse and snapped it shut. She had no real need of it. Sooner or later, a train would arrive.

She did not mention these visits to Alphonse. She didn't need him knowing all of her business. He came over every Saturday like clockwork to trim hedges or patch the back fence or some such thing she hadn't asked him to do. When she got back from the train station, she could hear him bumping around upstairs. She fixed him sardine sandwiches with mayonnaise and a wedge of onion, his favorite, and called him down for lunch.

They sat at the table in her little kitchen, and she drank her weekly can of beer, which she had on Saturdays, while he ate.

"Ma, you sound just like Gina," he was saying with his mouth full. He stuck his finger inside his cheek to adjust something, then he went back to chewing. "You know I ain't ready to be marrying nobody. I'm giving the girl everything she needs right now, so she ain't got nothing to be complaining about."

"By the time your father was your age, he owned a house and he was raising two children," Thelma said.

He gave her a sullen look she had come to know well and said nothing. Stripped down to his waist, clouds of white plaster dust covering his chest and his dark arms, he looked like he'd been baking bread. Except for the red bandanna he liked to sport on his head, hoodlum-style, when he was working. Finally he said, "I ain't trying to be my father. I ain't trying to be nobody but me, and it seems to me that ought to be good enough."

"Took you and your sister for rides out in the country. Took you kids to the baseball games every Sunday."

"You think I ought to be watching a game instead of running around here cutting the lawn and trimming the hedges on the weekends? Something wrong with me trying to help you out?"

Let him be, Thelma's good sense told her. He's doing the best that he can. He was so much like Earl to look at, with those dark hollows around his eyes that made him seem a little more banged up than the next person. That seemed to toughen Earl, gave him a kind of hard, extra layer, something that Alphonse, in his rumpled bandanna and baggy jeans, never had.

Alphonse looked up. "'Sides, it was Mr. Greavey who taught me everything anyway. Tagging up and squeeze plays and all. That was Mr. Greavey."

He was staring at her, not straight on, but in quick little flickers as his eyes moved back and forth between her and his plate.

"Mr. Greavey?" Thelma said. "That old wino probably spent all his time *under* the stands."

"He was sitting right next to me every game, Mama," Alphonse said, then he laughed to himself and looked off out the window. "Pops never went in much for baseball."

He got up, put his plate in the sink, and left her sitting there. She decided she'd go ahead and have a second can of beer and sat sipping it for some minutes, mulling over what her son had said. He always had some excuse. She took another sip of the beer and let it seep through her. If she let him, Alphonse would be a dried-up bachelor crawling around on her roof when he was ninety, making sure all the shingles were straight. She got up and went halfway up the stairs.

"Alphonse!" she called.

Something fell over, then there were stumbling sounds as he rushed out of the room he was in, and she realized that he'd taken the sharpness in her voice for alarm. He stood in the doorway, rigid.

"I want you-all to come over," she said. "For dinner, you and Gina. Next Saturday you be sure you bring her with you."

Several times during the next week, she walked down to the station and stood in the long hallway at the back from which the stairs led down to the tracks. Through the windows, she watched the incoming trains from far above. Most of the people getting on the trains went unescorted, with no good-byes and nobody to wave to from the windows. Nobody carried baskets of food along for the ride. People who got off did not even look at where they had arrived before they scampered up the stairs. It was a shame. This was no way to travel, not the way she had taken the train rides Earl used to give her, and she barely kept herself from banging on the windows with her fists to make these people look up and around.

She might have lingered for some time had not the two men shown up again, this time near the doors that led down to Tracks 1 and 3, running their mouths and taking even bolder glances at her now. They looked slightly familiar to her, but she didn't want them interrupting her, if that was what they had in mind, so she pushed open the nearest door, which led to Track 5, and took the stairs down.

At trackside she sat on one of the metal platform benches, all of which rested in the cool shadow of the hulk of the station a level above them. The first time she had looked up at the station like this she had been twenty-three, and though she had lived in its vicinity for all her life she had never taken a train before, and so had never seen it from this angle, and it had scared her. It had looked like a fortress, even though she'd just passed through it to get down to the tracks. When the train had pulled up, belching great drafts of steam to announce its arrival, debarking passengers jostled her out of their way. But Earl had come back for her, swept her up with one of the same big gestures he used to pepper his speech, and guided her through the streaming, chattering crowd. If it had not been for Earl, if he had not pulled her up the stairs into a car, she would have missed the first ride of her life.

After the long flight of stairs, her legs trembled. Not big tremors, just tiny ones that ran like static-electric shocks through her calves and thighs. Thelma took a tissue out of her purse and wiped away the film of sweat on her forehead. She didn't want to be sitting there shining like a greased pig when the next train came in. She patted her wig and straightened the skirt of her dress so it fell evenly over her knees. But instead of a train, she saw the two men a floor above her, looking through the windows above Track 5 into the distance over her head, as if they saw something coming she could not yet discern.

The following Saturday afternoon, with Alphonse banging around on the roof, she decided to walk down to the train station just to get away from all the noise, which got on her nerves even if it was necessary. When she went out the front door she found him looking down at her from the top of a ladder that leaned against the gutters at the roofline. He had on work gloves black with debris from the gutters, and he held a gardening trowel in one hand as he paused to ask where she was going.

She called up to him that she was going for a walk, and he called back down for her to wait. He descended the ladder and, with a flick of his wrist, threw the trowel like a knife into the dirt. Then he took off the gloves.

"Why don't I go with you?" he said.

"You don't need to do that," she replied.

"Where you going?" he asked again. "You planning to visit someone?"

"I thought you had your hands full here," Thelma said. "Wasn't that supposed to be it? Too busy for a decent dinner?"

He pulled the rag off his head, sighed, and wiped his face with it. "Gina didn't want to come."

She had already started to walk off when he said, "What am I supposed to do, drag her over here? She said you get so busy meddling all the time she can't hardly get her food down."

Thelma turned around. "What? What did you say?"

But he wouldn't repeat it, and he turned around and went back up the ladder as if he hadn't said a thing.

At the station, sitting on one of the trackside benches, she lost track of time. She did not believe that Gina had said such a thing. Gina and Alphonse had been together on and off since they were both in high school, with this last stint of five years being their longest. Gina had said, more than once, that she wanted children as soon as she and Alphonse were able to get married and afford a house. Certainly the girl had not changed her mind about that? Certainly she, at least, would not put up forever with Alphonse dragging his feet and keeping her around like she was some kind of—

"Earl's lady," said one of the men who'd been watching her. The two of them had come down to the platform while she wasn't looking. "It's you, isn't it?" he grinned.

They must have known Earl, Thelma realized. The tall, gaunt man was unfamiliar, but the one who spoke, the shorter one, shod in the thick-soled shoes of a janitor, almost brought someone to mind. He was very dark, with a small, almost pretty mouth. Earl had spoken of a "Lazy," or something like that, whom he reminded her vaguely of.

There was no way to avoid them now, so she gave him a polite smile and said, "Yes, yes I am."

"I knew it," he said, laughing, and elbowed the taller man sharply. "I said, gotta be her. Gotta be her. You was never the kind of woman a man was gonna forget. How you been?"

"Oh, I—I—fine, I guess," Thelma said, though she didn't like his manner.

"Well, I'm glad to hear it. I'm sure you remember me—Lacy. This here's Sil Carter. C'mon over here and meet—Patricia, right?"

Thelma opened her mouth, but nothing came out. Lacy's smile faded, and Sil Carter looked down at the concrete walk. In the awkward silence, Thelma finally found her voice and said, speaking the words very clearly, "Mrs. Thelma Stewart."

"Oh yes, oh yes," he said, and turned away looking slightly abashed. "Mrs. Thelma Stewart, yes."

The heat, along with everything else, just then became too much for her, and she put one hand to her bosom to steady the shallow breaths that no longer gave her enough air. She wanted the two men to leave. There was no reason, no reason at all, why they should be trying her when she was only there for the same thing that anybody ever came down to the station for: to visit a place only the trains could take her.

"You know, we miss him too," Sil Carter said, and his arm moved as if he might touch her shoulder, but he put his hand in his pocket.

"That's the truth," said Lacy, looking off down the tracks.

They didn't leave. Instead, they started to talk about Earl in vague terms, the way they might have if each was unsure they and

Thelma were thinking about the same man. Thelma listened politely, nodded at them and muttered the occasional "Oh my" or "You don't say." This went on for some time, until Thelma found she was breathing easily again, adding a longer comment here and there, letting herself smile along with them. The men seemed to relax too.

"You remember that time he got his tonsils out," said Sil Carter, "and here he is back at work the next day, and he pulls that old hip flask out like he always do. And he takes a sip and his eyes light up like he just set himself on *fire*."

He and Lacy cracked up, and Lacy said, "You couldn't keep him down long, though."

"Nuh-uh."

"No sir. Had to be running with all them friends of his. Had to go visiting them. He took me up in them hills in Highland one night, black as pitch back there, not one light, driving round in Sam Witherspoon 'n them's car half the night, and never did find the place he was looking for."

"Prob'ly drove right past it a hundred times."

"Wouldn't surprise me!"

"But he knew all them people back up in there."

"Everywhere! Both sides of the river, too."

"Every man, every woman."

For a moment, nobody said anything.

Then, "You-all worked with him, laying rails?" Thelma asked.

"Oh, yeah," Sil Carter said quickly, "and repairing 'em, summer and winter. It was some hard work, I'm telling you."

"Hard work," Lacy echoed.

An announcement over the P.A. system drowned Lacy and Carter out for a moment, and Thelma watched the people rushing toward the stairs to the tracks to meet the incoming train. Then it was quiet again.

"You remember that time," Sil Carter said, combing his fingers through what was left of his white hair, "he found that simple girl out there wandering around on the tracks?"

"What?" Lacy asked, then he said, "Oh, that one flying her scarf around like it was some kind of wind sock?"

"Yeah," Sil Carter said, "she just walking along with this scarf," and he waved his hand and stared at it as if something were flowing, rising and falling, from his fingertips. "Wouldn't never of heard a train coming, I'm sure."

Here Sil Carter paused, and he and Lacy looked at Thelma. This she had heard about before from Earl, though she'd never really thought about it, and she nodded at the men. "He took her up to the station," she said.

"Her family was up there," Sil Carter said. "Didn't even know she was gone."

"He was like that," Lacy said. He threw a grin at Sil Carter. "You remember when he got that old Plymouth, how he was just taking everybody—"

Just then an inbound train let out two long, hollow blasts of its horn, and the weight of it arriving sent a vibration up through the floor as it pulled into the station. Thelma smoothed down the skirt of her dress where it had wrinkled across her knees and wondered about the effect of all those trains coming and going, all that shaking of the foundation. Would it be possible to figure out if you could get enough trains, after a while, to make the whole station break loose and slide down the hill?

When Thelma noticed them again, Sil Carter and Lacy were sidling away, but not so obviously as to be rude. Lacy walked with a slight limp, she now saw, and Sil Carter squinted into the distance, as if he could see only poorly.

"Got to be going," Lacy said. "Nice talking to you, ma'am."

Nobody had called her that in years. People just didn't talk like that anymore now. Once she had reminded herself of that, she thought well of this Lacy for doing it.

Not long after they had met, when they had talked a few times, just enough to know that there would be much more to talk about later, Earl gave her the tickets.

She had spread the tickets in her smooth, limber, twenty-three-year-old's hands. They were for the following day, a Saturday, when school would be closed and she would not have to be at the first-grade class where she'd just started as a teacher's aide. That Saturday she had stood with Earl on the tracks as the train pulled in and a conductor in a cap swung himself out from an open door like some sort of trapeze artist. Earl pulled her up into a car, led her to a seat, and settled her in beside a window. She was wearing her best dress, a blue cotton one with a white sailor's collar. There was a tiny stain on the collar, but she had covered it carefully with white shoe polish the night before.

He leaned over the seat in front of hers and smiled at her. The off-white linen of his suit jacket curled and folded softly around the bends in his arms, and he smoothed down his little Cab Calloway mustache with his index finger. His slim hazel eyes studied her.

"You're traveling, sugar," he said.

"We're not even moving yet," she said lightly, and looked out the window as if to assure herself of it.

"People are always moving," he said. And then he told her about some of the things she was going to see, West Point, and Pollopel's Island, and maybe one of those big old freighters flying the colors of some foreign country.

The train lurched suddenly and stopped again, and Earl swung out of the seat he'd been in and kissed her on the forehead. He took a step toward the door.

"Well, where you going?" Thelma laughed. "You act like you're getting off the train."

He gave her a look of mock amazement. "What you think? Poor man like me can afford this kind of luxury for himself?" He paused a minute, then he was peeking around the edge of the door, doffing an imaginary hat. "I'll come for you when the train get back in."

And while she sat there, too astonished to speak, he jumped off the train just as it started to surge forward.

A few weeks later, Earl gave her tickets again. And there were more rides after that. In time she traveled to Albany too, on a northbound train, past little towns in brick and shingle, below hills where ruined mansions were just visible behind the trees. She became an assured traveler. She tipped a porter once for carrying her coat on a day that turned very hot between morning and late afternoon. She came to remember the order of the stations, and sometimes answered questions—Does the train stop at Fordham? What time do we get to Yonkers?—for other passengers. At the end of each trip, she waited in Grand Central or the station at Albany until the train back home was ready to depart. One time, coming back from New York, she waited in her seat while all the other passengers left the train and watched Earl scamper back and forth impatiently along the platform, looking for her. She sat there for quite a while. He'd put on a cream-colored fedora with a sea-green band since she'd left him, and she could not take her eyes from it.

They'd kept it up briefly after their marriage three months later. Some of the people, the ones who rode the trains or frequented the stations, became familiar to her. There was a man, a very old man whom age had deepened and darkened like wood, who often sat on a bench in the Winnikee Falls station with his cane held like a tiller where it balanced between his knees. He wore a black suit, and nodded to her each time she passed. A black woman her age sometimes rode to Albany with three white children who called her "Nanie." "Nanie, I want the crackers." "Nanie, I have to go pee." They seemed not to know the words "please" or "thank you" even though they were older than the children in her class, and sometimes Thelma thought that if they were in her charge, she would have a conductor come by one day and scare them by telling them they had to get off the train, alone, far from home. But this was sneaky, and she knew it, and so she stopped thinking about it.

Another woman, older than Thelma by a few years, often got on at Winnikee Falls just as Thelma was returning. She was just plump enough to be solid, and over her processed hair wore small, fashionable, tilted hats that matched her dress or coat. She neither looked up nor around her as she boarded, and nobody saw her off. Once she came into Thelma's car before Thelma had gathered her things to get off. Though she hadn't bumped Thelma, hadn't touched her at all, she said very clearly, "Oh, I'm sorry," and paused for a moment. Then, looking a bit embarrassed, she made her way farther back in the car.

And now Thelma knew her name. Patricia.

After that ride, Earl had told her that he had run through his free tickets, and as much as the fellows in the station liked him, he was not likely to get any more. He left the railroad at the end of the year for a job driving a delivery van. Those rides had done as much for Thelma as they ever would by the time they ended, and she thought she would not miss them. But she did.

The ticket girl told her the same thing, and so did the station manager, a large, fat man who wore a navy-blue vested suit with a watch chain hanging out of the vest. He looked to be about thirty years old, with short blond hair trimmed as close as a crew cut.

"We plant a memorial tree for your husband," the man said, fingering the chain, "we're gonna have to plant a hundred more. Half the people in this city got relatives connected to the railroad."

"How many of them saved somebody's child," Thelma asked, "from being hit by a train? Seem to me that's a pretty big thing."

The idea had come to her after Lacy and Sil Carter had left her. She had seen a story on the TV news recently about a local elementary school planting a tree to remember a little girl who'd been killed, and it came back to her. She had spent three days thinking about it, dismissing it as silly, burning with it as if it were Necessity itself, but mostly swinging in long and tiring arcs between these two extremes.

"Probably a whole—" the man said, and then, apparently thinking better of it, said, "That's not the point."

She'd found Lacy that morning and gotten him to confirm the story to the station manager, who had listened to the whole account fooling with his watch chain and looking off around the room as if he had better things to do.

"Look, let me show you something," the manager said, and he turned and walked briskly out the front doors.

When Thelma made it outside, he was standing over by a bench, looking down at the little plot of grass next to it that she had told him was the spot she wanted.

"Now, you see this?" he said, pointing at the ground. "This here? People come over here for a smoke, where do they drop their butts? Right here. You don't want that."

Thelma stood looking at the grass, where a handful of cigarette butts lay among the tangle, along with a piece of a cigar.

"And the last thing we need is to get roots growing into the wall here, specially around this window," the manager continued. "And we got some pipes running through here, too, and the root system would get all tied up in there, we'd get leakage. You don't really want to cause all that trouble, do you? What kind of memorial would that be?"

Thelma looked up at him. How easy it was to talk to this man, about whom she cared not a whit. "I'll call up the nursery and find out what kind of tree is best to fit this place," she said.

The station manager scratched his jaw, said something about looking into it, and ambled back into the station.

Off in the distance, she could just see the choppy waters of the Hudson, the dull gray of it blown into whitecaps by the day's erratic breeze. She sat down on the bench to rest a moment before going home. She hadn't told Alphonse anything yet, but now it was time she did, she decided, as she rose to leave.

Alphonse wasn't yet there when she got home. Thelma went inside and watched television for some time while she waited for him, but the day wound on and he did not come. Usually on Saturdays he came during the late morning and stayed until mid-afternoon, and it was already past two o'clock. She lifted the remote and flipped through all the stations on her cable system, but nothing held her attention and she turned the television off.

She rose and wandered the ground floor of the house. Earl was with her, of course, in every room. There, on the wall, was the shadow of the old hat rack, where he would sling the fedora when he came in and where it nestled against the wall until, wearing the right suit, he would lift it off with an index finger as he went out. And here, at this table, he'd sat spearing his scrambled eggs with a fork as he questioned her minutely about the children and their schoolwork, their health, their need for new shoes, their daughter's getting into fights, their son's habit of breaking things, and more and more, all dumped into the space of his not coming home the night before. There had been too many of those nights, too many through the years. And fights. And trousers and shirts draped over chairs, strange perfume seeping from their pores.

She slowly climbed the stairs and made her way down the hall to the spare bedroom. The wall was still bare of paint where

Alphonse had repaired it. She could find no trace of the crack that had opened there. She ran her fingers over the dried plaster, feeling for it, but she met only a smoothness, nothing to catch her fingertips on. How would she ever get him to stay away, to lavish his flood of devotion where it would do him some good?

The slamming of a car door drew Thelma's eyes to the window, which looked out on the street in front of the house. Alphonse was getting out of his car. He walked around to the passenger side and opened the door for Gina, who emerged quickly. She put her arm around his waist, and he did the same around hers, and they marched halfway across the street, laughing and staggering, until they nearly fell and had to let go. Then they merely walked the rest of the way in easy unison, nodding and speaking to one another, until they disappeared under the roof of Thelma's front porch.

Their feet clattered up the stairs. Thelma waited to hear Alphonse's key in the lock, turning the bolt. Several seconds passed. Then, through the house, rang the church-bell chiming of the front doorbell.

In the end it took about six weeks for Thelma to prevail. She wrote to her state senator, asking for his help. All he offered was a long-winded letter full of phrases like "dedicated service" and "civic pride," but when she sent it along to the railroad people, it was enough to get them to do what she wanted. They scheduled a small ceremony and planting for a day in late August.

After the date was set, she did not go back to the train station. She set out several times to do so, but fatigue overtook her, and she made it only as far as a nearby playground or corner store before turning around to go home. Once she had to call a taxicab to carry her back, so hard had it become for her to breathe in the late-summer heat. After this she decided to take her walks back up into the neighborhood, which had changed greatly and was changing still. Some of the old frame houses had been torn down, and in their places were empty lots of packed dirt where you might find a sofa or a car on blocks. Others had been freshly painted in colors more muted than the original reds, blues, and greens, and had new doors inset with small windows, and small plates with the street number alongside the doors. She found she could walk about this way for an hour or more, even in the sun.

The night before the day, she called a cab to take her to the station. She could have called Alphonse, but he and Gina would be there in the morning for the planting, and there was no point in bothering him to go twice. The cab let her off around nine-thirty, when most of the cars had left the lot and only the occasional person passed through the station's doors.

There was just enough light to see the tree, its roots bound up in a piece of heavy burlap secured with rope, leaning against the wall beside a hole in the plot by the bench. She walked over and peered down into the blackness of the hole, which appeared bottomless in the dim light. She ought to have brought something to throw into it, but she hadn't had the forethought to bring anything, and when she went through the contents of her purse, nothing that was what she wanted presented itself. She had a few pictures in her wallet, old and faded, and somewhere in the bottom was the ring Earl had worn from the day she met him until the day she slid it from his dead finger. She had been not quite fifty then, but she had felt, for months afterward, as lost as she had at twenty-three.

A year or so after he had died, she had finally sought a transfer to another school from Innis Elementary, where she had been teaching first grade. It took her two years to secure it. At the new school, Platt, her second-grade class had somehow discovered on what day her birthday fell and surprised her with a party not long after she arrived. They brought in home-baked sugar cookies still gummy in the centers, mashed cupcakes, and candy in half-full bags. She had played records on a turntable, and they danced and ate everything. They drank disgustingly sweet Hawaiian Punch out of plastic cups, and when the pipes started to clank, signaling a premature blast of heat from the cranky furnace that would bake them well past comfort during the coming winter, they opened all the windows. Teachers from other classes drifted in and out, telling her, *Welcome.* All afternoon they surrounded her, the faces of children she did not yet know, all of those new voices laughing and shouting and, from time to time, speaking her name.

She touched the bark of Earl's little tree. With her toe, she nudged the tight bundle of roots in the sack. The nursery people had assured

PASSAGE

her that this type of maple, a dwarf variety, would cause no trouble to the pipes and walls of the station. Hardly grows at all, they had said. But looking at the narrow fit, she could see what they could not have imagined: branches bent by the hard brick walls, roots straining against the cold metal grip of those underground pipes. Yes, she could see it as clearly as if it were happening right now, in front of her, without any years of waiting at all. She snapped her purse shut and went inside the station to call a cab.

SAINT SEBASTIAN STREET

Beatriz makes no effort to listen for Grace, who sleeps without making a sound. In the first-floor nursery, that stuffy room converted from a pantry or sewing nook, she breathes so silently you would think she were dead if you did not know her ways.

Grace doesn't call Beatriz "Nanny," or "Mrs. Franklin," or anything else. She does a noise in the back of her throat, something between humming and the sound you might make inadvertently while puzzling over a question: *hnnnnnnn.* She stops it when Beatriz comes to her or, if already in the room, picks her up. Upon first hearing it Beatriz thought, *This child is an animal.* The adoption agency must have found her in the forest.

In fact, Mrs. Oglethorpe told Beatriz on her first day of work, Grace came from a family with a mother and a father, southerners, maybe Appalachians. But burdened with many children, they could afford no more, and so Grace became Mrs. Oglethorpe's blessing, her ray of hope after years of trying to conceive and then more of trying to adopt. Mr. Oglethorpe's pride and joy. A small blond angel promising them a new rightness in the world, Beatriz understood.

Through the open kitchen window, a breeze enters and lifts the yellow curtains. Beatriz goes back to her novel, but eventually she puts the paperback face down on her knee. It is a serious, literary book, a novel well-reviewed by critics, the story of a sheltered housewife who meets and falls in love with a dwarf traveling with a carnival. Luella is the housewife's name. Hilo, the man's. He is ebullient enough to sit on her lap after hours, uninvited, and tell her ribald tales that win her heart. Beatriz closes the book without inserting the marker. She is not going to finish such a silly story.

Mrs. Oglethorpe drives up, revs the motor of her Volvo to a roar, holds her foot to the pedal for a moment—*whirrrrrrrr*—and cuts the engine. Then it is quiet again, until Mrs. Oglethorpe bursts through the back door dragging two shopping bags that make a huge racket as she piles them onto the small kitchen table. Unlike Beatriz, who is short and the color of walnuts, Mrs. Oglethorpe is tall and blond as sunlight, almost six feet of radiance. Beatriz can imagine her skirted and aproned, frolicking among flower gardens in the Alps. There is enough of her to make two or three Heidis at least. But this is unfair, of course. Mrs. Oglethorpe and her husband are of English background, reserved and most of the time polite.

"You're home early," Beatriz says. Noncommittal. Her day is now disrupted.

"I had a little time between meetings," says Mrs. Oglethorpe, and she pats the bags nervously. "I brought a few toys for Gracie."

The job had been Raymond's idea, her husband's flash of inspiration the night Beatriz told him that she'd been turned down for yet another office job she'd interviewed for. All the rejections, she couldn't understand it. Why not try one of those child care arrangements, he'd said. It would only be temporary. Honest, respectable work, just a way to tide her over till she got an offer. People in their neighborhood, along Prospect and Whitney and Orange and all the streets in between, were so desperate for nannies that they put up posters on trees and lampposts, begging for help.

Desperation. It was not the way she had imagined finding a job. She could not picture herself in the place of the young women, barely more than girls, whom she saw pushing strollers with squalling white babies up and down the streets. Their mouths crooked, full of English words too feeble yet to serve them, their eyes betraying thoughts in Spanish, of even less use to them now. Beatriz had grown up a few hours away, in upstate New York, and had lived in New Haven through eight years of married life. Had been to college, had worked in the office of Raymond's sportswear company. She was not cut out to be some matron's wet nurse, muttering *Yes'm* and *No'm*, melting into the walls when she was dismissed.

Even so, the first poster she answered produced an interview.

Sitting there in Mrs. Oglethorpe's sun-hazed living room the same afternoon she'd telephoned, Beatriz found herself growing dizzy with confusion. The more she admitted her lack of qualifications, the happier Mrs. Oglethorpe became.

"No," she said, "nothing. Not even baby-sitting."

Mrs. Oglethorpe laced her fingers across her knee and smiled broadly. "But you've been to college."

"Yes, I have a bachelor's degree from the University of Hartford."

"In what area?"

Beatriz hesitated. "Physical anthropology."

"Oh my," said Mrs. Oglethorpe, and she laughed. "Would you like some coffee?"

"No thank you," said Beatriz. She didn't wish to delay finishing this and getting out the door any longer than necessary.

"And you didn't want children of your own?"

Beatriz rearranged her scarf, picked a mote of lint off her navy skirt. When she and Raymond had first married, he had told her he wanted no children for a while. His resources had to go into his new business; he did not want the drain. Later they would have them. And being twenty-two, fresh out of the university, very square and practical in her desires, trusting that time brought progress, she had not disagreed. But none of this was the business of the woman sitting across from her, watching her with the intentness of a thief examining a window left ajar.

"My husband and I have no children," she simply said.

"Marvelous!" said Mrs. Oglethorpe, leaning back into the cushions of her overstuffed couch. For a moment she just breathed heavily. Then she said, "When can you start?"

"Start?" Beatriz echoed.

"Oh, first let me show you the baby," Mrs. Oglethorpe said, and she rose and led Beatriz through the big house, from back to front, until near the kitchen she turned in to a small room bathed in shadow.

There was a white crib in one corner, with a mobile of fish and birds pushed back from it, so that the animal figures were mashed against the wall. In the crib was no baby, though. Beatriz did poorly at guessing children's ages, but she would not have called this one a baby. Her bare legs were fully formed, ready for walking and running. She was old enough to speak.

"This is Gracie," Mrs. Oglethorpe whispered.

She seemed anything but desperate, then, this woman, as she rested her hands on the railing of the crib. The dim calm even soothed Beatriz's nerves. She compared the long parade of all her rejections to this one family, the single pair in front of her, and the balance tipped before she even checked her math, before she wondered if there was some hidden weight that might even the scales.

After Mrs. Oglethorpe gave Beatriz her initial set of instructions, run off on her laser printer at work, she left the running of the household pretty much to Beatriz for a while. Then, in the mornings before she left for work, and in the evenings when she came home, she began to give more niggling little bits of direction. Don't put brown sugar in Gracie's farina. Don't forget to make her wash her hands both before and after she eats.

"Don't braid her hair. It pulls her scalp. Look at how it makes her scowl."

"That's not a scowl," said Beatriz. "She always looks like that."

Gracie sat across the kitchen table from them, flipping through the pages of a coloring book she'd shown no desire to use her crayons on. Sixty-four Crayolas sat pristine in their box at her elbow.

Mrs. Oglethorpe frowned. "Just leave it loose, Beatriz."

"Okay. I'll take the braids out tomorrow morning, pronto."

"Never mind. I'll do it myself tonight."

Mrs. Oglethorpe walked Beatriz to the front door.

"And Beatriz, please don't speak Spanish to her," she whispered when they were out of earshot of the kitchen.

"What?" said Beatriz.

"She's having enough trouble talking as it is," said Mrs. Oglethorpe. "I don't want her to get confused."

Beatriz looked at her. What on earth was the woman thinking? Was it the word "pronto" that set her off? Beatriz's name? She hadn't said a thing about her origins to Mrs. Oglethorpe.

"I do not speak Spanish," Beatriz said stiffly.

She'd been born in Puerto Rico, but her father had brought her back to his home in the U.S. when she was four. Her mother had died in childbirth, and her father sometimes said that four years of his wife's family, which had never been fond of the black man from New York who married their Magali, was more than any man should have to take. Beatriz had no memory of them, nor of the island, or the language. She knew only a few words that anyone living in the continental U.S. would recognize: *mañana, amigo, siesta. Dinero. Hasta la vista.*

She was tempted to use this last to bid farewell to Mrs. Oglethorpe, but she decided to keep it to herself.

Mrs. Oglethorpe—Mrs. O, as Beatriz calls her, less out of familiarity than to ease the load on her tongue—pulls the two huge shopping bags open and, after rummaging noisily through one of them, takes out a portable Nintendo and a board game in a colorful box. Grace, Beatriz is certain, will not touch either of them. From the other bag Mrs. O pulls an enormous white polar bear, larger than Grace, with a black nose and black eyes and daggerlike felt claws.

From the nursery, there is a sound of stirring, then Grace begins her drone.

Mrs. O's eyes flash at Beatriz, an unmistakable look of desperation.

"You've woken her," Beatriz says coldly, and rises to go to the nursery.

It's not her job to provide comfort to this fluffy woman, and she won't. Her job is to cook and feed, to read stories, play games, take walks, and coo lullabies, and for Grace she competently provides all of the services for which she is paid. And paid no great salary. She is not inclined to throw in extras.

But Mrs. O stops her in the hall with a hand on her shoulder. "I'll go," she says.

And with the bear clutched to her chest like a shield, she goes into the nursery.

Beatriz waits just outside the door as Grace continues to drone for several minutes, never modulating her tone, consistent as the seasons. Then her pitch changes, and she gradually grows quieter until, suddenly, she falls silent. Beatriz hovers. Minutes tick by.

Beatriz cannot believe the evidence of her ears. She hesitates, puzzles, and finally resolves to look around the doorjamb. Grace appears to be once more asleep. She is pressed up into the fur of the bear, nothing of her visible but the small arm that encircles the thing's neck. Child and bear are squeezed into the foot-end of the white crib in which she sleeps, well away from Mrs. O and out of her reach where she sits, in a chair, at the head, her hands balled together, her eyes bright.

"See, Beatriz?" she says, smiling, in a low harsh voice. "You see?"

The girl is exhausting. It is not that she fusses, argues, or resists Beatriz's will. Rather, the child floats free in her own world, from which it is necessary to yank her over and over for such simple things as eating, sleeping, even playing.

"Gracie. Gracie. Gracie," Beatriz says.

The child looks up from the bear, whose ear she is twisting as she sits on the living room floor behind a wing chair.

"It's time for your nap. Come on now."

Grace picks up the bear, which looks to be losing its stuffing, and drags it down the hall.

It hasn't taken long for the thing to become a comedy of filth. Grace carries it to the back yard, to the landing of the stairs where she perches for hours, to the toilet. And then to bed.

"Gracie, you have to let me wash it," Beatriz insists later, gently tugging.

She doesn't remember when she picked up the "Gracie" business, but it seems the thing to do now, to talk affectionately to the girl to cajole the bear away from her. Wasn't that what one did with children? She'd had so little contact with them. Though she would not have admitted it to Mrs. O, she had come to think of them somewhat like pets, small beings of limited mental powers who required periodic feeding and a warm place to sleep. Perhaps this was why she had not pressed Raymond on the subject. But Grace clutches the bear as if she doesn't hear. And Beatriz still is not even sure that if she got the bear away from her it would fit in the large-capacity Kenmore washer that waits for it down in the basement.

And then one day, when Grace bangs in through the screen door trailing the bear, a veil of weeds hanging from its head, a big, dark badge of dirt on its stomach, Beatriz turns from the stove where she is warming soup, determined to get the bear loose from the child, and succeeds in doing nothing but collapsing in helpless laughter.

Grace turns around and runs back out of the house.

Beatriz sighs and goes back to stirring. This is not going to be easy.

That afternoon, when Grace's nap is over and she's had her cup of milk, Beatriz tries to send her out to play. Perhaps it is a bit regimental, but she is sure that fresh air and sunshine are a necessity for growth, so Grace gets a dose of each every morning and afternoon. Maybe it will even help her mind; Beatriz has started to wonder if anything will, short of professional intervention. Mrs. O believes that she will come along, open up, be ready to start kindergarten in the fall. But Beatriz has her doubts.

"Go outside and play now," she tells the girl.

Grace stands at the back door, silently gazing out into the yard, a messy collage of collapsing trellis, overrun herb garden, and Adirondack chairs disappearing into the knee-high weeds. Beatriz has stopped wondering why people with money like the Oglethorpes' let their property fall into such a state.

Grace doesn't stir.

Beatriz realizes that the bear is gone. Did Grace, lost in some reverie, forget it and leave it somewhere? Out in the weeds, or under her parents' bed?

The child is staring at her when Beatriz glances down, expecting to see the head full of mustard-yellow curls. Then Grace pushes the handle and steps out into the sun.

An hour later Beatriz has found no sign of the bear. Not a button eye, not a claw. Not one tuft of acrylic fur.

After Mr. Oglethorpe has left for his job—he is some sort of human resources administrator—Beatriz brings up something she wants to discuss with Mrs. O: the crib. In the two weeks Beatriz has cared for Grace, she has grown convinced that it has to go. It's too small for the child, and the railings, even when down, make it necessary for her to be put in and out of bed like a baby.

"She's small for a five-year-old. She hasn't outgrown it yet," says Mrs. O, gulping coffee between words. "I've got to go."

"It's designed for an infant. Just like the mobile. How is she ever going to learn to behave like a normal child if she can't even get in and out of bed alone?"

Mrs. O recoils as if she's been slapped. Then she draws herself up to her full height.

"Maybe you just don't want to pick her up."

"That is ridiculous!" Beatriz says. "If I—"

From the living room comes the sound of Grace droning. Beatriz leaves the kitchen with Mrs. O following her. Grace, wedged underneath the glass-topped coffee table, stops as soon as they enter the room. She has her cheek pressed against the glass, distorting her face into a pancake-sized splotch with one dark eye peering up out of it.

"Come here, honey, and kiss Mommy good-bye," Mrs. O croons.

Grace climbs out and sits on the carpet. Mrs. O gives her a lingering kiss on the top of her head and dashes out the door.

Eventually, though, she relents, and the delivery van arrives with the bed a few days later. After the men from the store have brought it in, they ask if Beatriz wants them to dispose of the crib.

"Yes," she says immediately, though it is not hers to send away.

But Grace refuses to go near the new bed. When Beatriz calls her for her nap, she comes in and touches it, walks around it, examining the rainbow and clouds on the headboard, and finally stands staring at it. Nothing Beatriz tries coaxes her onto it. Nothing short of lifting her bodily and plopping her down on it is going to work, Beatriz realizes. And that won't make her stay.

So Beatriz climbs in herself. It seems a good way to lure the child in: show her there is no harm, that it is safe. Her head scrapes the rainbow, and her feet, when she kicks off her shoes, touch the footboard even when she bends her knees.

When she wakes up, Grace is wedged against her, breathing deeply.

Beatriz checks her impulse to leap, embarrassed, from the bed. Grace lies sleeping beside her, nestled strangely against the curve of her back. From this close Beatriz can hear her breathing, feel it through her ribs, and she lies there briefly as the motion moves through her like a tide. Then, slowly, she begins to separate herself from Grace, careful not to wake her. And as she performs this slow uncoupling, the dream she had comes back to her. A man, an old man in a Panama hat and gray hair showing at his unbuttoned shirt collar. Sunshine, saltwater air. *"Eh, niña,"* he is saying. *"¿Dónde está la calle San Sebastián?"*

She is a child, gazing up at him. She must answer him, because he is an adult, but she does not know the answer and her aunts have wandered off from her, as they sometimes do for a while among the fruit stands and baskets, and she has no one else to ask. But she spins around anyway, looking, until the world becomes a blur.

That is all she remembers.

She doesn't bring up the dream to Raymond. Over dinner, instead, Beatriz tells Raymond of Mrs. O's latest inanity, and he says, "Well, why don't you quit, then?"

"El Viejo," her father used to call Raymond when he wasn't around, that summer after college before Raymond and she married: one of the few Spanish phrases in which he indulged in Beatriz's presence. *Old man.* His way of reminding her that Raymond was ten years her senior, too old to date his daughter.

"Just give it up," Raymond says, buttering a slice of bread.

"But it's only been a month," Beatriz says. "I can't give up so soon."

Raymond chews. He is a dark-skinned man, large-headed and spare of body, formal in his movements. He handles his fork like a fine-tipped paintbrush, as he handles everything he touches.

"I have to go away for a few days. Los Angeles. There are some people interested in the new children's line."

In the early years, Raymond would bring business associates to their apartment, and Beatriz would cook elaborate dinners for them from books: veal marsala, chicken cordon bleu, Hungarian goulash. Dressed elegantly, she would chat about any subject that arose. Raymond would often fall silent and watch. But he'd long since taken to courting his clients in restaurants, and traveled on business alone now. Hectic, he would say if she asked about his trips; she wouldn't want to come. Besides, even with Rose, he needed her in the office. So she stopped asking, and had not started again when, a year ago, she decided she'd spent enough time there.

"Are my suits back from the cleaners?" he asks. "The blue one, I mean? You know, the one with the funny buttons?"

"You should retire that thing."

"What do you mean?"

"How old is it, Raymond? It looks like disco fever."

Raymond looks offended, then he smiles.

"It's not that bad."

"Yes it is."

He wipes his mouth with a napkin, leans back in his chair, and sighs, gazing at her intently but with the smile still playing about the corners of his mouth.

"All right, then. Throw it away. Break my heart."

Beatriz gets up and clears away the dishes. Then she comes back and massages Raymond's shoulders.

"Umm."

"Do you really think I should quit?"

"Why not? There are a hundred jobs just like it that you could have instead. Why bother keeping one that you don't like? You could try another one."

"I guess so."

"Or you could come back to the office," he says. "Rose is going to be leaving soon. Maternity leave. I could use you there, Beatriz."

Beatriz stops her hands moving. In the early days it had saved a lot of money, her taking phone calls, filing, keeping books; helped to get the business off the ground. After that she had just—no sense in avoiding the word—lingered. For lack of a better idea, a new vision of herself that, try as she might, she could not summon to mind. Those long hours and reams of figures, the endless minutiae, they were dull but sheltering. A harbor. She was needed there, so she had belonged.

"But I hardly remember—" she begins.

"Just think about it, that's all," he says, nodding slightly. "No pressure. Honest." Then he looks up at her, and the playful look on his face makes her smile until he says, "But really, wouldn't it be better than chasing around after somebody's brat all day?"

"Gracie," Beatriz says. She has just wrestled a basketful of laundry up from the basement, and thinks better of kicking the door shut behind her. "Gracie. Gracie, honey."

Gracie sits at the table, pushing the pieces of a colorful wood puzzle around the slick top in random motions, forming nothing. She doesn't look up from what she is doing.

Beatriz glares at her, then sighs. It is a form of play, surely. A private game. Who knows what she is thinking?

She puts down the basket, shuts the door, walks over to Gracie and leans over her shoulder. Gracie keeps up with the puzzle.

Beatriz puts the laundry away. When she starts lunch, Gracie is still there, sliding the pieces. Perhaps Raymond is right, she is a hopeless brat. But who knows how she lived before she came to Mrs. Oglethorpe's cavernous, echoing house? Perhaps she is simply accustomed to smaller, more intimate spaces. Perhaps the presence of all those people around her, all those brothers and sisters, was not such a bad thing after all and, relieved of the pressure, she has lost her original form, become misshapen.

She has wondered about herself. Of Puerto Rico, what was left for her? Little more than her name, as far as she can tell. She finds no romantic trace in the loss, no affinity for seawater or ocean vista, no flash of parrot blues and yellows at the edges of her daydreams, no taste for the meager flesh of the big-seeded mangoes she's picked up once or twice in Stop & Shop. Poor fruit, they'd been; poor nourishment for any kind of hunger. And even her name is a weak link. *Beatriz*. Until she was fifteen and found her real name in a box of documents in the attic, her father had called her Bibi. Exclusively. A term of affection, he had labeled it, and how could she get angry over that?

And as for the dream about Saint Sebastian Street—she looked up the words and translated them into English—she doesn't know what to do with it. It came to her only once, in that half hour as she slept beside Gracie in the child's bed, and returned no more. Beatriz feels some relief that it has not recurred, become some nighttime haunting she can neither understand nor escape. And yet the brilliance of the picture, the clarity of the words, has not faded a bit from her mind.

After lunch Beatriz sends Gracie to wash her hands and face and sits at the table, thinking. She's made up her mind that she will decide, today, about whether or not to stay. While Gracie is outside playing, she will have plenty of time to mull the question over, and she looks forward to the peace and quiet, because so far she has gotten nowhere with thinking, has gone round and round in circles.

Outside, the sky has darkened. Clouds have been scuttling across it all morning, but now they have thickened and lowered. There is no sense in sending Gracie out to get soaked. When she comes back, ready to be sent out to play, Beatriz runs through the options for filling a two hour block of the child's time: stories, puzzles, dolls, coloring books, television.

Gracie is staring at her. She's wearing a yellow sundress and white socks and sneakers; Mrs. O has taken to dressing her before Beatriz arrives in the morning. But she never looks quite right, so Beatriz makes little changes here and there. Today she pulled Gracie's hair up into a ponytail, tying it in a turquoise ribbon after she had given the rough frizz in the back a good, straightening brushing.

"What do you want to do?" Beatriz asks her.

She expects no answer, but there's no harm in asking.

Gracie looks at the floor.

Beatriz sighs. Rain starts to spatter the kitchen window.

"Do you want to watch television?"

Gracie shakes her head, just perceptibly, No.

"Well, well. Do you want to play with your coloring book?"

Again, and more clearly, No.

Beatriz crosses her arms. "Let's play a game."

Gracie nods, Yes.

"Yes, really?"

Yes.

She's staring up at Beatriz, the blue of her eyes shifting to browns and grays in the rainy gloom. Beatriz never turned on the lights when the sky clouded over, and now the house is as shadowy as a cellar. But Beatriz pays no attention to this, so absorbed is she in finding the right game to keep Gracie engaged. No hopscotch in this weather. The Nintendo and board games Mrs. O bought for Gracie are still in their plastic wrapping, dumped in a closet. There's little else around, not even a ball and jacks, or a deck of cards.

"Hide and seek," Beatriz says.

Gracie doesn't break her gaze.

"You count to ten while I go and hide. Then you try to find me, okay?"

Gracie nods.

"Close your eyes."

She doesn't count out loud; her mouth doesn't even move, but as Beatriz watches her she knows Gracie is marking increments of time, somehow. Beatriz hesitates, trying to grasp the method, but her time is running out. She dashes into the living room and crouches behind a wing chair.

Her legs start to burn from the strain almost immediately. She cannot hear Gracie moving, and wonders whether she has left the kitchen, has even understood the game. But the next instant she is standing beside the chair, smiling shyly. *Found you.*

Beatriz rises and gives her a hug. "That's my good girl," she says.

Gracie smiles and backs away into the living room, and stares intently again. It is almost unnerving to Beatriz after the many times she has nearly had to shout just to get Gracie's attention.

"Again?"

Yes, again.

Beatriz wishes Gracie would say more. Just a little more. Then she laughs at herself, because this makes no sense, of course. Gracie hasn't said anything to add to in the first place. But Beatriz abandons this thought, because Gracie is counting again, and Beatriz scurries up the stairs. This time she hides behind the bathroom door, but like the first time, Gracie is beside her almost immediately.

"You're good! You're so good!" Beatriz says.

She cups Gracie's face in her hands. Soft cheeks. Gracie rubs one of them against her palm.

"This time you hide, okay?"

Yes. You find me now.

Beatriz closes her eyes, counts to ten. When she opens them, she is in the bathroom alone. And her heart has been pounding so strongly that she has missed the clue which she realizes Gracie must have been using all along: the sound of feet moving away from her.

She steps out of the bathroom. Rain patters gently against the windows outside. She feels along the wall for the light switch and turns it on. A faint glow rises from the wall sconces planted among the brown mahogany borders and doors. A cursory glance into the upstairs rooms produces nothing, as does a quick tour of the first floor. Beatriz thinks of calling out to Gracie that she'll find her, that she's coming. But this seems to be more for her benefit than Gracie's, so she abstains.

She searches the ground floor again: nothing. And nobody in the back yard, which is to be expected, since the door is latched from the inside.

Upstairs, she checks all the rooms a second time, even searches the master bedroom closet and peers under the bed. There is an attic, reached by a narrow, shadowed stairway at the end of the hall, but Beatriz is certain Gracie would not venture inside. It's creepy even for an adult, and the door sticks. She stands at the top of the main stairs, listening for sounds of Gracie moving.

There is only the patter of rain.

She hurries down the stairs. In her purse, on a folded envelope, is the phone number where Mrs. O may be reached at work.

"Gracie! Gracie!"

Beatriz stands in the kitchen, breathing heavily, trying to push from her mind the thought that is forcing its way in. Not a fear that Gracie has fallen, that she lies injured, that a knock on the head has left her unconscious. Not this child. Wherever she has gone may lie beyond Beatriz's ability to follow—beyond the bounds of her thin imagination.

The basement.

She flings open the door, throwing it against the wall with a loud *thwak,* and plunges down into the semidarkness. The light switch produces only a faint glow. Beatriz looks in the washer, and in the dryer, but they are empty. Deeper in, piles of plywood bearing rusted nails, used paneling, a stack of doors, a claw-foot bathtub. But no Grace. Beatriz brushes cobwebs out of her hair and runs back upstairs to the kitchen.

It takes her eyes a moment to readjust.

Gracie is peeking from around the edge of a counter, smiling.

Beatriz steps forward, leans toward Gracie. Words tumble out of her mouth. She grabs Gracie by the arm and slaps her on the back of her bare legs, hard, before she can stop herself.

As soon as she has done it, Beatriz wishes she could take it back. But of course she cannot. Gracie's face crinkles, and her eyes well over with tears. Beatriz sinks back against a counter. She cannot even begin to explain to this child what has happened, why she has overreacted, ruined everything in one paranoid instant, and she waits for Gracie to commence the awful, unbearable droning again. But after she has wiped her eyes with the back of her hand, Gracie stands staring at her.

"I'm so sorry," Beatriz finally says, when she can summon the breath.

She cannot tell what Gracie is thinking. Outside the rain has risen to a steady downpour. In the rainy gloom, Gracie's mustard curls, yellow sundress, and white sneakers have drained of color, making her look like an afterimage of the girl she was. Her unblinking eyes are black. Beatriz is the one to finally break the stare between them, dropping her forehead into the palm of her hand and wringing the skin there with her fingers. With her head down, she works up the gumption to speak and is about to open her mouth when she hears something that amazes her: Gracie skipping off down the hall. Up the stairs she gallops, through one and then another bedroom she runs, plunking down on her knees and banging doors as she goes. Finally Beatriz hears her pound into Mr. O's den right above the kitchen and settle abruptly. And then, quietly, patiently, she waits.

That evening, Beatriz resigns her job. It's just a formality, given the faint pink mark that has bloomed on Gracie's thigh. Mrs. Oglethorpe takes one look at it and screams—a small, choked scream, but a scream nonetheless—before she gets a hold on herself, throws her arms around Gracie, and covers her with kisses as she flashes looks of fury at Beatriz. Through it all Gracie sits at the kitchen table with her box of Crayolas, calmly working on what might be huge animals or brightly colored mountains.

Nothing Mrs. Oglethorpe could do, however, would make a dent in the shame that weighs Beatriz down as she walks home. Her hand tingles still, as if it is offering itself for the only just punishment: being cut off. As she walks along the twilit street, she sees the latest round of child care posters tacked up onto trees and lampposts, their ink streaked into long filaments by the rain earlier in the day. They're illegible now, mute appeals for help that nobody could understand. As she walks along, she pulls them from their places and collects them, so that when she passes through her own front door and finds Raymond watching television, the mass of them drips in her hand.

He wants to know what she's carrying, but she doesn't explain, just wanders into her own kitchen, throws them away, and begins preparing dinner. Frozen cauliflower. Black-eyed peas from a can. The pork chops she transferred from the freezer in the morning so they would thaw during the day. As she places a saucepan on the stove and upends the can, dumping its contents into the pan, she knows only one thing for certain. She is not going to be able to eat any of it.

Raymond manages nicely. When Beatriz tells him what happened at the Oglethorpes', he is full of sympathy, at first, but this soon gives way to his worry that the Oglethorpes will file some sort of lawsuit. "That English girl, that Louise Woodward, who killed that little boy," he says as he chews. "And that case in Stamford, the swimming pool accident. Used to be people watched each other's kids all the time, no big deal. Now it's dangerous."

Beatriz puts down her glass and leaves the room.

She goes to bed. So tired, bone-tired, she can bring herself to do nothing more than crawl under the covers, still fully dressed, and fall into a sleep so deep that time seems to detour around her. When she awakens it is broad daylight, Raymond has risen and left for work, and she is alone.

There is nothing to do. After breakfast, Beatriz sits staring out the window, watching the traffic moving purposefully up and down Whitney Avenue. She could put on her shoes and go wandering about the neighborhood, but she has never been the wandering type. She has never felt the urge to strike out from home, not just to see what the day might bring her, but to look at the houses and sidewalks and trees and cars and see *something*—like a painter with a canvas would. Something that has not just been handed to her by other people. No, all she would be able to do is head straight for the big yellow and white Victorian she has come to know so well. Stand out on the front lawn, stare at the curtained windows. Wait.

You find me now.

Sitting against the headboard, her clothes twisted and rumpled, her eyes caked with crumbs of sleep, Beatriz hears it, hears Gracie, as clearly as she hears her own breath. But is it a memory? Is it her imagination? And how can she hear a language that has never been spoken?

Three days pass and Friday arrives before Beatriz decides what to do.

She slips past the Volvo in the driveway. The presence of the car tells her that Mrs. Oglethorpe hasn't yet found someone new to work as her nanny, but Beatriz doesn't care. The job is not what she has come for. Through the portal of the collapsing trellis she goes, then into the high grass and behind one of the moldy Adirondack chairs. She's on her hands and knees now, and she feels the dampness of the dirt and the bugs crawling around beneath her, all that life so far below her usual threshold of notice. The earth vibrates down here. She could roll around in the grass, fill her slacks, her blouse, with blades and burrs and ants and spiders. She could throw rocks at people, and they'd never know who did it. She scoops up some dirt, presses it into a ball, then squishes it into a warm, heavy mud pie.

It is not long before the screen door shimmers. Beatriz peers through the slats of the chair's back as Gracie kicks through the door, comes down the stairs, wanders into the yard. One foot on the first cracked slate of the decorative walkway, one foot on the next, and the next.

And then she sees Beatriz.

Beatriz holds her gaze for a moment. Then growls long and low.

Gracie laughs and runs forward.

YEARBOOK

They find her in the tall grass near the Elm Haven housing projects just before sundown: Denise Freeman, lying in the weeds along the old Northampton–New Haven rail line. She's dressed in filthy denim overalls and a grimy, tattered T-shirt, wears a sky-blue bandanna around her shaggy head and thick-soled, cherry-red flip-flops at least a size too small on her feet. She was beautiful once, but only her honey-tan skin, improbably smooth after twenty-some-odd years of living like a tramp, hints at that now.

There's no smell yet, nor many bugs around, just a few gnats that circle lazily above her in the August heat. Rain from the morning has beaten down the denim, making it look like a rag hugging a rock. She has stiffened into a bashful pose, with her head turned way to one side and her right hand flung up by her face, the fingers curled around. An empty Fritos bag nestles close to her left knee.

Tiffany Spottswood and her friend, Keisha Taylor, simply stand there looking at their discovery for several moments. "I'm a get my mother," Keisha says, and runs off without another word. Tiffany gets a stick. She pokes Freeman in the side, and the stick snaps as if she has thrust it against a brick wall.

She tosses the broken piece of stick into the weeds. Briefly, she wonders what has become of the shopping cart full of junk she's seen Denise Freeman pushing up and down the streets. Then, because dead or alive, Freeman is just Freeman to her, chattering to herself, yelling nonsense at people who are minding their own business, picking through the trash in people's back yards like she is arranging tomatoes on her salad, Tiffany's mind wanders from the figure on the ground at her feet. There's a new pair of shoes waiting for her at home, burgundy platform sandals, the first heels she's ever had, and come this weekend she will get to wear them to her mother's church's talent show, in which her cousin will perform Fats Domino's "Blueberry Hill." She doesn't give a damn about her cousin's performance, or care all that much about the hopscotch game she was setting up to play with Keisha. Right now it is the burgundy shoes that haunt her. But a tiny sliver of light just beneath Denise Freeman's chin catches her eye. She steps closer. She forgets the shoes, summons her nerve, and reaches out to part the folds of fabric where the light is half-hidden.

Keisha returns quickly with her mother. Mrs. Taylor, who is known by all adults, including her husband, as Mrs. Taylor, clucks softly at the sight of Freeman. She just stands there looking, as the sun drops, for quite some time, until Keisha pulls on her arm to remind her mother she is there. "Go tell Mrs. Parry," she tells her daughter, and Keisha, possessed of a fearsome energy, tears off at a gallop on her new assignment. When the pounding of her sneakers fades, Mrs. Taylor bends over, thrusting her behind in the air, and sticks one hand down the front of Freeman's shirt. Tiffany holds her breath for a moment, wondering what Mrs. Taylor is doing. Mrs. Taylor unhooks the shoulder straps of Freeman's overalls and yanks the shirt up; the bib she rolls down in a ball until it will go no farther. "Uh-hm, no underwear," she says. She puts the shirt and bib back loosely.

Mrs. Parry takes her time arriving. The day is folding up to go when she finally gets there, a brown paper grocery bag clutched in one hand.

"Good," says Mrs. Taylor, reaching for the bag. "I was hoping you'd think of it."

"I'm not stupid," Mrs. Parry says, withholding the bag.

She's a small woman, big-eyed, childless though you would think she had a passel of children at home. From the bag she pulls an A-cup bra and a pair of flowered panties.

"You get those offa some baby doll?" Mrs. Taylor says.

"I got 'em at American Discount, same place you get yours, thank you."

Next she takes out a polyester blouse with a ruffled collar and a pleated, tweed skirt.

"Ruth, it is the end of August," Mrs. Taylor says, looking at the clothes.

"And is she going to complain? Can we please get started?"

It takes them a good twenty minutes, by which time it is dark. Freeman turns out to be as unyielding in death as she was in life, and providing her with her last change of clothes is a struggle with her rigid limbs. Two or three people gather behind Keisha and Tiffany as Ruth and her friend work.

"I heard sometimes these funeral home people have to break an arm or something," Ruth says as she stands up, finished.

"Really?" Mrs. Taylor says, standing also.

"Only way to get 'em to move the way you need to put on the clothes."

"It's true," says a voice behind them. Mabel Hodge, who has buried two sons in the last five years.

Just then there is the sound of car tires on gravelly earth, and a police car with its light whirling pulls up near them. The doors swing open, and two officers approach Freeman and her entourage.

One of them shines a flashlight over her.

"Not this one again," the cop says.

"She's dead," Mrs. Taylor says.

"Dead?" says the officer. He steps around to where he can see better and runs the beam all over Freeman, as if some particular part of her will confirm the report. "What'd you move her for?"

Since it is self-evident, nobody answers him.

The cop snatches his hat off his head in exasperation. "You had to move her around and all this?"

His partner, in a uniform that is slightly too big for him, hangs back in the shadows near the car and watches silently.

"It's only gonna make it harder to figure out what happened to her."

Mrs. Taylor laughs humorlessly. "We already know what happened to her," she says.

The talent show goes off without a hitch. Tiffany's cousin takes first prize, and when Tiffany can take no more of the ritual of incessant purring and petting that her cousin and her adult admirers fall into after the show, she slips away.

She and her skinny self and the platform shoes wander unnoticed among all sorts of adults, most of whom she knows and a few she does not recognize, absorbing the gossip they do not even notice she is drinking up. As long as she keeps her mouth shut, adults mostly go unaware of her presence, something she long ago learned to exploit.

Mr. Hedges, for example.

"Same old shit. Same old shit as before," he is saying to another man, the two of them flanking the stairway that leads up from the basement all-purpose room to the first floor. "Lost half the blood in his body, and he lying there in that hospital bed telling me he don't regret none of it, not a bit."

"Hardheaded," the other man, elderly and stooped, says.

Tiffany moves on. She's heard enough before about Mr. Hedges's stupid son. Working the room, she gets the lowdown on who got her hair burned off by a bad relaxer, who's got a bunch of little dogs he doesn't take care of, who broke into Eval's rib place and got stuck in that tiny alley window trying to get away.

Then she finds herself off in a corner with three old ladies in Sunday finery, though it is only Friday night. They can always be counted on to attend events for "the young people," with whom they have little but wishful thinking in common. They have, apparently, exhausted all topics related to their doctor's appointments and church activities by the time Tiffany finds them and have worked their way around to Denise Freeman.

"I bet she was out there hooking just like she been doing for years," says the first, who is wearing purple. "One of her customers decided he didn't get his money's worth, I bet."

"But she wasn't beat up, they said," another chimes in. "No more than usual, anyhow. Looked like she was sleeping."

The third turns her withered face down toward her plastic cup of soda before she speaks. "Probably just her high blood pressure caught up with her. You can't play around with that."

"Well, she gone to her maker now," says purple, and from the tone of her voice Tiffany can tell this is not the usual good word for the dead.

The second is chewing her lip, as if she actually knows something she may or may not want to tell. Tiffany watches her: a woman with bulges under the clingy fabric of her floral dress, in a wig just a touch askew and a pillbox hat with a wisp of veil.

"She used to say she wouldn't get nowhere near those tracks. She used to say they was dangerous, still dangerous, and they needed to fence them off," she finally offers.

The other two look at her. Clearly, they have nothing from the horse's mouth and know they've been trumped. But purple gathers herself, unwilling to be silenced by so small a thing as a lack of knowledge.

"Ain't been a train on those tracks in decades," she announces.

"Well, who don't know that?" the third asks.

Denise Freeman knew it perfectly well, they all seem to understand; and just like that they move on to Reverend McAlister's daughter's husband's souped-up car. Loud as hell, just what Dixwell Avenue needs every Saturday morning.

Tiffany can do nothing. They won't go back to what she wants to hear, they will not explain a thing, and if she asks them anything they will shoo her away. Her power lies in secrecy and stealth. It is, really, an unsatisfying kind of power. She stares at that soft pastel pillbox with its delicate veil and feels a pang of desire; she wants it.

Just then Keisha skips across the floor and collides with her. *Wham!* Tiffany could slap her, but Keisha is giggling and pushing her toward the stairwell, and her spirit cannot resist the pull of Keisha's frenetic good humor.

"Well, what?" Tiffany laughs as they carom past Hedges and his audience of one. Up the stairs they go.

"Let's get out of here," Keisha says, and before Tiffany can answer, her friend is out the front door.

Several weeks later, Tiffany sits at the back of Mrs. Glaser's fifth-grade classroom. The high, venetian-blinded windows let the sounds of the street leak in a bit, but not enough to drown out Mrs. Glaser's voice as she drones on about the Roman Empire. Tiffany drifts. Mrs. Glaser is now talking about reading the newspaper. It is August-hot still, though it is now late September, and Tiffany would like to faint from the heat. A girl did that last year, during a performance of the fourth-grade chorus, while everybody was standing on bleachers on the auditorium stage and singing. Fainted and fell off. Nobody's seen her in school since.

"Now, who can you interview? Right? Who is going to be a good person for you to do for your interview? Rodney?"

"President Reagan," Rodney says.

Mrs. Glaser does one of those not-really-funny laughs she thinks nobody understands.

"Well, Rodney, he's kinda hard to get ahold of, so he's not too good. Who else?"

Sheila Titus. "Grandmaster Flash."

Some of the students giggle at this. Tiffany picks a wad of bubble gum out from under her desk and places it, like a ball of pizza dough awaiting the chef's touch, on the surface of her desk.

"Who else?" Mrs. Glaser asks. "Come on, people."

She's stalking back and forth across the front of the room, making the kids who were shortsighted enough to sit up there in the first place squirm. Her red hair looks like a fire against her pale skin, and her dress swirls as she goes.

"Everybody, it doesn't have to be somebody . . . famous," Mrs. Glaser says, pronouncing her words carefully. "It can be somebody you know, right, somebody who is doing good work in the community. Now who can you think of?"

Tiffany raises her hand. A look of relieved anticipation comes over Mrs. Glaser.

"A derelict," she says.

"A . . . derelict," Mrs. Glaser says. "Hmm. Well."

Tiffany pushes the gum into points of a star as she waits for Mrs. Glaser to respond. Three, four, five points stretched out so thin they could snap at any moment.

There's a dictionary on Mrs. Glaser's desk, but Tiffany knows she is not going to pick it up.

"A derelict."

Tiffany nods.

Mrs. Glaser leans against her desk, near the dictionary, and runs her fingers along the clean plastic desktop. "That's one idea," she says slowly. "Now, who else?"

She has two weeks to finish what Mrs. Glaser has innocently set in motion. She can make most of it up herself since she's seen plenty of Denise Freeman's crazy theatrics in her short life. But the problem is, though she'd like to spice her "interview" with a few nuggets of fact, nobody wants to tell her anything.

"Who you think I am, Miss Jane Pittman or something?" one elderly neighbor sitting out on her porch tells Tiffany when she comes halfway up the stairs with her steno pad at the ready. "You couldn't give me the time of day before, and now you want to talk to me? Go on."

Mrs. Thomas next door says, "You go and ask your mother."

When Tiffany catches Mrs. Parry trudging home with an armload full of groceries, she just says she doesn't want to talk about it.

"Why not?" Tiffany says.

"Girl, can't you see I'm busy!" Mrs. Parry snaps, and moves on.

Mrs. Parry, of course, is always busy. For somebody with no kids and no husband anymore, now that what Tiffany's mother refers to as "that common-law man of hers" is long-since dead, she is busier than she has any right to be. She is always rushing somewhere, always has her face screwed up with some plan. Sometimes Tiffany would like to tell her, *Hey, lighten up.* Today, in fact. At least Mrs. Parry isn't chasing around after some ghost nobody wants to talk about.

Tiffany is sitting outside on the curb, watching cars go languidly by, watching the boys in a lot of them, thinking she might as well go interview the Korean guy who runs the corner store or a librarian or someone equally dull, when Mrs. Taylor comes along, minus Keisha.

"Well, hello, Tiffany," she says.

"Hi, Mrs. Taylor," Tiffany says in her best voice of defeat.

"What's bothering you?" Mrs. Taylor says.

Her tone is more businesslike than sympathetic, but that's good enough.

"I got this assignment I gotta get some help with," Tiffany says.

"Well, they got afternoon tutoring over at the Center, you know," Mrs. Taylor says.

Mrs. Taylor has funny eyes, light-colored though her skin is dark, bored into her head, intense. Tiffany looks at the sidewalk, picks up a twig and starts tracing out letters spelling nothing in particular.

"Not like that. I'm supposed to write about that bum lady that died, but nobody wants to tell me anything."

"Why you want to write about her?" asks Mrs. Taylor.

It's the last question Tiffany is expecting, and she can't help but smile. "I don't know," she lies.

It doesn't get past Mrs. Taylor. When Tiffany looks up, Keisha's mother is glowering down at her like a thickening storm, and she wipes the smile off her face at once.

"You wanna know about her? You take your butt on down to New Haven Free Public Library and look her up. They got newspapers going back some years. You such a good student, you shouldn't have no trouble at all."

And with that, Mrs. Taylor wheels and stalks off. Tiffany floats in a hot flush of humiliation for a few moments, then she gets up and brushes off her jeans. She doesn't like the implication that she ought to have known what Mrs. Taylor said. Who would think to look in the library to find out anything about somebody like that? In fact, she suspects it is just a busywork errand from yet another adult who seeks to withhold information from her. It is some kind of conspiracy, clearly.

But she goes anyway: down Dixwell Avenue, past the buildings, the shabby and the new, that she's known all her life, down through Yale's dingy gothic towers, to the New Haven Green. She enters the public library, finds a librarian to help her—the one adult who's given her a hand so far—and soon she is whirling away at a micro-film machine, tracking down the day in 1940 when Denise Freeman was born.

It takes Tiffany a while to find it. From the two-line death notice in the *New Haven Register,* she gets only the year of Freeman's birth. When she turns up the birth announcement in a November issue of the *New Haven Journal-Courier,* it is so brief she nearly misses it. Denise Freeman, daughter born to Flora Jenkins Freeman and

Harold Freeman, businessman and owner of Swanky's Starlight Bar and Restaurant. The newsprint is grainy, the years seem an impenetrable veil. The time is too other, too far away from what she knows, for Tiffany to grasp at first the implications of money and social status in maiden names and eating establishments with high-life pretensions.

That only starts later, as she lies in bed that night, listening to the pipes in the ceiling clank as Mr. Hunter, the upstairs neighbor, washes up to go to work. Swanky's Starlight Bar and Restaurant. The name is weird, funny on her tongue, impossible to connect to the Denise Freeman she knows. The newsprint grain gives a new texture to the once-simple darkness that crowds her bedroom. She can feel it. Never, really, has she been afraid of the dark—as her cousin still is. It has hatched too many fine things in her brain for that.

But there is not much more to be found, and the little the librarian helps her turn up is boring anyway: Swanky's sold and torn down for urban renewal, Flora Freeman's obituary coyly shrouding the cause of death in syrupy phrases that make her sound happier than she ever was in life. The librarian clucks apologetically and disappears.

When she gets home around dinnertime, her mother tells her that Keisha was around looking for her. Tiffany flips on the TV and plunks herself down on the couch. It is some dumb show she has no real interest in, but she watches it anyway. She hasn't seen Keisha in half a week, days she has spent grubbing around in microfilm and boxed archival material and tedious books of awards and business reports and church histories. Her research skills now would rival those of a college freshman, though she doesn't know it. Neither such matters nor the bitterness of her lack of results occupies her mind at the moment.

"When did she come?" she asks her mother, who is in the kitchen.

"'Bout an hour ago," her mother replies.

An hour of Keisha wondering where Tiffany is, when she'll return, whether they might get in a game of hopscotch before dark. Tiffany rolls all that unrequited desire around on her tongue and feeds slowly on it until her mother calls her in for dinner.

Another two days pass before Tiffany lets Keisha find her at home.

Keisha's there on the threshold, looking like her wild-child self, when Tiffany opens the door at her knock.

"Where you been?" Keisha says.

Her hair's standing out around her head, her clothing's askew, and her eyes are unblinking. It's almost enough to make Tiffany shut the door, this maniac who is her best friend.

Keisha grabs her and hauls her out the door.

Tiffany has to run to keep up. Down the block they race, across Dixwell Avenue against the light to the accompaniment of honking horns, down another block past a razor-wire-fenced lot.

"Wait *up!*" Tiffany finally gasps, and pulls up short before her heaving chest can burst. "Where the heck are you *going*?"

Keisha spins around, laughing. "Girl, you so slow. Come on."

They walk a few doors to an auto-supply place on Whalley Avenue, where Keisha buys some spark plugs her father has sent her out for. Then they walk back toward Keisha's home, heading down a street that will take them, for the first time since they found Denise Freeman, past the spot along the train tracks.

There is not a bent blade of grass, not a trace. Keisha treads around as if her feet can pick up clues on their own.

"You want to see something?" she asks.

"Yeah," Tiffany says.

She won't ask what. She can't believe Keisha knows something she doesn't, not after all those questions she asked people and all that time she spent in the library. So she follows Keisha down the weed-choked, rusting tracks, denying all the way that anything having to do with Denise Freeman awaits them.

Keisha stops at a big platform of concrete like an overgrown sidewalk square separated, somehow, from its kind. It looks funny out there in the weeds. Huge cracks run through it, breaking it into five or six pieces. A rusted metal loop protrudes from one of the pieces.

Keisha wraps her hands around the loop and pulls with all her might. The concrete piece shrugs and lifts slowly until Keisha has managed to pull it entirely upright. Tiffany steps closer. The bottom side of it is covered with swarming ants, masses of them running crazily in all directions.

It's just another Keisha freak show. Tiffany groans. Her friend stands there, balancing the slab, holding onto the metal ring long past the point that Tiffany would have dropped the thing out of disgust at the swarm of ants. She looks at Tiffany and grins. And still she hangs on while the ants seethe and writhe until they seem a thing come to life.

Finally, she drops it. The slab falls back, but out of alignment, so that when it hits the ground it cracks against another slab and shatters into powder and many smaller pieces. The ants scatter: into the grass, across the rest of the concrete, in both directions down the nearest rail in two rolling columns.

As one column heads in the direction of the spot, Tiffany's skin begins to crawl. She remembers her mother's hysterical reaction whenever she finds an ant, one lonely ant, anywhere in the apartment, as if it is the lead scout of an invasion. The brooms, shoe heels, sprays, and powders she attacks with. Her mother has come to terms with silverfish and roaches, those constant companions on lower Dixwell Avenue, but ants she cannot abide.

Tiffany turns around and stares at the spot where they found Denise Freeman. *You had to live outside with them things,* she imagines her mother saying, *you'd be talking to yourself too.*

Mrs. Glaser stops her as she is leaving school on a Friday afternoon. She pulls Tiffany back into the classroom, out of the dingy hall the other kids are filing through on their way out of the building.

Tiffany doesn't mind. She likes the creaky old school, always has, from the rubber cement she used to peel off the big, round tabletops to help clean up in kindergarten to the stairwell out back where she took furtive glances at boys peeing, leaving the treacly smell of that hidden place she love-hates to this day. She is happy to linger late, have more of the school to herself. Tiffany waits while Mrs. Glaser talks to somebody in the hall before coming back to her.

Mrs. Glaser smiles a something-in-mind smile. "Tiffany, how would you like to be an editor?" she asks.

Tiffany shrugs. It's a familiar word, but one empty of experience for her.

Mrs. Glaser looks disappointed, but she presses on. "Some of the teachers thought it would be nice for all of you to have something to take with you when you leave for middle school next year. A yearbook. Have you ever seen a yearbook?"

"No," Tiffany says.

"It's like a scrapbook for everybody," Mrs. Glaser says.

She reaches over to one side of the desk she is sitting on and pulls several large, rectangular books out of her tote bag.

"Take a look through these," Mrs. Glaser says, standing. "I'll be right back. I have to talk to Mrs. Broadhurst for a minute."

Tiffany opens the first one—a Wurtsville, Pennsylvania, class of 1969 tome done up in embossed maroon faux leather—before Mrs. Glaser has even finished speaking. Every last person in the book is white. Everybody in the cafeteria, the gym, the classrooms, everywhere, is white; she has never seen such a concentration of white people in one school, and it sets her to musing about how different Pennsylvania must be from Connecticut. There are small pictures of all of the students that go on for pages and pages. They smile, smirk, glower, look at the camera, look at nothing, hide behind the glare of a flash against the lenses of their glasses. They all look uncombed, sloppy beyond belief, even Mrs. Glaser, who peers out of a tiny photo in the "Juniors" section. The face is younger, for sure, but the eyes, nose, and mouth definitely belong to Mrs. Glaser.

She looks up. Mrs. Glaser is gone.

There are two others. The one from Poughkeepsie High School in New York State, 1978, she puts aside in favor of the other: Hillhouse High, 1958. Hillhouse High is where her cousin will go the following year. Tiffany has seen it a million times from the outside, all its wise, nonchalant, older students milling around on the stairs, caught up in conversations and affairs she can't begin to fathom. All she could do was gawk. Now she has a door to the interior. She opens it slowly.

Candid black-and-white shots of people dancing, bending over pieces of artwork, sitting in class, and standing in clusters in the halls make up the first five or six pages of the book. Then there are the activities: the theater club in costumes, the band holding their instruments, all these group shots carefully captioned: *l. to r., front row: Miss Millie Potter, Miss Mimi Pitts, Mr. Eldridge Higgins . . .* Many

of the last names are ones that she recognizes from the neighborhood. She searches for Mrs. Taylor, Mrs. Parry, or her own mother,
but finds only other people she knows vaguely: Mr. Hughson from
the car-repair shop near school, Mrs. Fitch from the church, both in
barely recognizable portraits of their younger selves. Tiffany flips
more pages. All of the people are black, but they wear clothes she
would expect to see white people in: girls in wide skirts and sad-
dle shoes, boys in cardigans and ties.

Finding the same pattern of organization as in the first yearbook,
she turns to the individual photos of the seniors. Each is accom-
panied by a quote and a list of activities: *Community Assistance, Student Alliance, French Club.* Ed Thompson, smiling from beneath a
razor-close haircut, says, "Onward and upward!" Carlise Whitaker,
Student Council and Communications Club—like many of the activities, a mystery to Tiffany—says, "Always put your best foot forward!" Tiffany flips one page, scans it, flips another.

Denise Freeman stares back at her.

Even with all that time subtracted from the features, she knows
the face in an instant, without even looking at the captioned name.
The concentrated darkness of the eyes, the hard line of the mouth,
these are the same, though the smooth pageboy curling under the
chin is new, even funny on that face. Everyone else is smiling;
Freeman is not. Her gaze at the camera is neither casual nor friend-
ly, but it isn't crazy either. And this hangs Tiffany up for quite some
time, because in her life she has known craziness as she knows hazel
eyes or a high speaking voice: as one of the markers that distin-
guish one person from another, as one's own indelible imprint, deep
and permanent. The idea that you could start without any of these
and acquire them had never occurred to her until now.

There is no quote. The blade of disappointment Tiffany feels at
this surprises her. She recovers herself and runs a finger over the list
of activities, which exceeds that of any of the other seniors in the
whole book. *Community Outreach, Student Council, Big Sisters, Committee for the Mayor's Day Celebration, Downtown Council, National
Honor Society, Spanish Club, French Club, Yearbook Committee Co-
Chairman, Math Society, Girl's Softball Captain.* Tiffany looks again at
the photograph, frowns, and sits back in her seat. Then she laughs

to herself because this is some kind of joke on her, obviously. The person in the yearbook, the baby in the birth notice, the shopping-cart lady, they couldn't possibly all be the same Denise Freeman, could they?

Mrs. Glaser is back suddenly, bustling through the door and talking as she comes. "Now, of course, ours is not going to be as elaborate as this but we do want to have some pictures and some articles about our school."

She pulls a rain scarf out of her purse and ties it around her head. Her red hair, full of static from the humidity, floats out of the scarf where it meets her head.

"You think about it, right?" she says, gathering up the yearbooks and stuffing them back in her bag.

Tiffany, speechless still, lets her take them.

"You think it's a good idea, don't you?" Mrs. Glaser asks. "The students will like it, won't they?"

She really seems not to know. Normally, Tiffany would just agree; agreeing with Mrs. Glaser cost nothing, whether you meant it or not, because she would forget in five minutes anyway. But today Tiffany has a not-so-sure feeling and she hesitates to speak.

"I don't know," she finally says.

By dinnertime Tiffany has thrown away the fake interview she had written for the next day's class. She has started and torn up so many "interviews" she has lost track of the number. What seemed like a joke, at first, has turned into a nightmare. She had planned to make up not only the questions she was supposed to be asking, but the loony answers Freeman would have supplied had she been alive to mutter them through her chapped lips. "Where were you born?" "I don't remember, it was a long time ago." "What do you do for a living?" "I do whatever I feel like doing." And so on. But this, Tiffany hears clearly every time she starts writing it, is just Tiffany talking to herself, and somehow she expects even Mrs. Glaser is going to catch on to that fact in about one minute. The problem is the other presence that Tiffany can feel gathering itself out of the bits and pieces of facts she knows—a presence now exerting itself against her silly concoction, showing the deformity of her bright idea, the utter falseness at its center. She cannot grasp the presence and make sense of it, but neither can she elude it.

And there is simply no way to just go through the motions, either, as she does normally when her homework starts to bore her. There is no simple, plodding version like the ones the other kids in her class are bound to turn in. There is no such option here. And it is too late to go interview somebody for real.

She gives up. She picks through the Green Giant kitchen-cut string beans, doctored with a little bacon, the sweet potatoes, and the homely lump of meat loaf her mother serves her at dinner. Then she's gone.

It takes her an hour to find Keisha, who is not at home. She's not at the spot near the tracks, the rusting playground, the auto store with the junk parts out back, up or down Dixwell. She's in the laundromat on the corner of Argyle Street, watching the chipped and peeling washers spin their foamy loads.

"Keisha!" Tiffany yells over the racket of all the machines.

But when she gets Keisha outside, she can't remember why she went looking for her. What is she going to do, ask Keisha to help her with her interview? Hardly.

They roam through storefront shops, chattering, picking over merchandise they have no intention of buying and annoying clerks and owners. In the course of thirty minutes or so Tiffany has shared enough of her travails for Keisha to know what is bugging her, and as they stand out on the sidewalk, fooling with the door of a mailbox, Keisha says, "I know what you could do."

"What?" Tiffany says.

"Go ask some of them other winos. They all know each other with their crazy selves."

Tiffany rolls her eyes. "Are you kidding? They don't even know what day of the week it is."

Keisha lets the door snap shut. "Fine. You surely got a better idea."

Tiffany does not. So she shuts up and follows Keisha, who treks over to the American Linen Company building. There, they slip around back and climb down to the railroad tracks that run past the building in a channel about a foot and a half below ground level. These are the same Northampton–New Haven line tracks

137

they found Freeman near, but this portion is farther south and less familiar to Tiffany. Here, the low walls are banked with red sandstone blackened with age and soot. Litter and weeds of every variety choke the area alongside the tracks. They head south.

The railroad bed plunges deeper into the earth. By the time they reach the place where busy Prospect Street passes overhead, the traffic of cars is so high and far away it sounds as muffled as a TV playing behind a closed door. At first the underpass that Tiffany and Keisha approach looks pitch-black. But when they get to its mouth, Tiffany can see the glow of light from the other side, and she follows Keisha's silhouette into the gloom. Still, it is hard for her to keep up, with all the bottles, rocks, and railroad ties she keeps tripping over, and Keisha reaches the far end first.

An overturned shopping cart marks the mouth of the tunnel. When Tiffany emerges, Keisha is sitting on it as if it is her living-room couch, waiting for her.

"Thought you freaked," she says blandly.

Tiffany brushes at her clothes. "Where are we going, anyway? How far is it?" She is not too keen on the idea of picking her way through junk for much longer.

"Just come on," Keisha says, and heads off.

The farther they go, the thicker the cast-off debris of other people's lives becomes. Shoes, clothes, a baby bathtub, a busted stroller. Car batteries, cushions, curlers, a toolbox, an ironing board, a dollhouse, most of it beaten to shades of gray by the rain and the sun. Tiffany looks up time and again, expecting to see people at street level about to toss old tires or raggedy clothes down on her head. But nobody does. And all the while that they keep marching, Tiffany on unsteady feet, Keisha with the assurance of someone who has been there before, it seems that they are getting farther away from the streets above, though they have descended no deeper than they were back at the Prospect Street underpass.

As Tiffany watches her friend scramble expertly over a mound of dirt that covers the tracks where a section of wall has given way, she feels suddenly tired, as if she has been unplugged from the energy of cars and pedestrians on the streets above. She leans against a wall, then pulls away when her clothes stick to it. Keisha crests the hill with the fluidity of a cat and scoots down the other side, out of sight. And Tiffany considers not following. Keisha is off on another planet, hardly even aware of her friend anymore, Tiffany is sure, and would not even notice she was gone.

"You coming?" Keisha calls.

The note in her voice speaks the rest: because we're down here for *you*. Tiffany sighs, crawls up the pile of dirt, and eases herself down the other side.

Keisha's standing a few yards away, at the mouth of another underpass. But with this one, Tiffany cannot see through to the other side. It is just a hole into blackness.

"We're not going in there," Tiffany says. "You could break your neck in there! You can't see a thing, Keisha!"

"You're not going to break your neck," Keisha says.

She doesn't explain why not. Tiffany plants her hands on her hips. "We ought to go around."

"There's no way around, unless you want to go all the way back to where we started," Keisha says.

There's no anger or impatience in her voice. She just waits.

"How do you know there's not some big hole or broken glass in there? Why didn't you bring a flashlight?"

"Tiffany, ain't nothing going to happen to you. You think I'm gonna let you get hurt?"

Let her get hurt? Up until that instant, it had not occurred to Tiffany that Keisha was directing anything but their route. Certainly not that she was Keisha's responsibility, as she might be her mother's, or Mrs. Glaser's. She squints at Keisha. Keisha?

Keisha gazes back at her levelly, turns around, and walks into the shadow of the overpass.

Tiffany scrambles after her.

It is quiet enough that she can hear Keisha ahead of her. They move along at a steady pace. Tiffany suspects her friend has deliberately slowed down so as not to leave her behind, and this gets on her nerves. But that passes quickly, so much concentration does it take to stay upright and with Keisha. The light behind them recedes.

"You okay?" Keisha asks.

"Yeah," Tiffany says.

And she is. She is, and she is thinking that they will soon be to the other side, when she collides painfully with Keisha.

"Ow!"

"Sorry."

"What'd you stop for?"

"Just a minute."

Tiffany's ears ring, and her nose hurts where she smacked it into Keisha's head, but she does as she's been told. The ringing and throbbing fade quickly. No noise of traffic, absolutely none at all, fades in to replace them. It is utterly silent. And then Tiffany hears a stirring some yards away from them.

Then a grunt.

Tiffany freezes. The darkness moves. She can't see it, but she can hear it, and it is coming from several directions all at once, so that she cannot tell what the individual directions are, or how many of them there are. Her breath just about stops, and her head locks in place where her ears pick up the maximum sound.

"Hello? Are you-all in here?" Keisha asks aloud.

Tiffany turns and gapes, blindly, at her friend. She knew this? She reaches out a hand toward Keisha, but comes up with nothing but air.

"I gotta ask you-all something."

"What'chou want, girl?" a woman's voice rasps.

Keisha's feet scuff the ground as she turns toward the voice.

"You-all knew Miss Freeman, right?"

There is broken, phlegmatic laughter from another direction. "She'nt get down here much. She'nt like it down here." It is a man's voice, crackling. "She'nt come unless she had to."

"She come, though?"

"Oh yeah, oh yeah." More laughter. "Wasn't too proud *lately,* oh no."

Without knowing what her feet are going to do, Tiffany bolts. Heedless of the hazard of tripping or the possible placement of bodies, she hurtles out of the underpass at such a speed that it is unlikely that even Keisha could catch her. And when she makes the light, she keeps on running. Up over the dirt mountain, down the other side, headlong down the tracks, kicking up a mighty spray of ballast as she goes, until the ugly, welcome brick of the American Linen Company looms just ahead.

When she gets home, she can hear her mother snoring. She shuts the door quietly, though as heavily as her mother sleeps it would take a bomb to wake her up.

Tiffany is filthy. She is not big on baths, but she strips and runs a tub of water, then slips in and slides down until the water is up around her neck. She is still shaking. The water is not hot enough. She has left every light in the apartment burning.

She soaps herself head to toe and rinses. Twice. She puts on a nightgown, pads to her bedroom in pink slippers, pushes open the door, and hesitates. She closes the door without going in.

Her mother is sleeping on her back in her own bed, sucking in great drafts of air as if she is drowning, letting them out again in chunky gasps. Her eyelids reveal thin crescents of white, and there are dried tears at the outer corners of her eyes. With her mouth open, her cheeks are slack and hollow, and the fat beneath her chin bulges. Tiffany has seen her mother sleep before; she is often catching a nap when Tiffany gets in from school, resting up for the night shift she often works at Caldor after her daytime shift in the same place. Overtime's good money, she will say drowsily over dinner sometimes, though Tiffany now wonders what is so good about it. Her mother snorts loudly and rolls over, and though Tiffany silently wills her to, she doesn't awaken.

So she raises the covers as much as she can—her mother has fallen asleep on top of the bedspread—and crawls underneath.

But Mrs. Spottswood's sleep remains a struggle, and Tiffany lies awake all night, listening, for the first time, to how it goes.

Mrs. Glaser asks her to stay again a few days later. While Tiffany stands before her steel-gray desk, she takes out the one-page "interview" that Tiffany handed in a day late and stares at it with an unreadable expression pinching her features.

"Tiffany, we both know how bright a girl you are," she begins, not looking at Tiffany.

This does not, somehow, sound as much like a compliment as it once did.

"But lately you seem to be having some attitude problems."

"Attitude problems?" Tiffany echoes, confused.

Mrs. Glaser gives her a sharp glance.

"This woman is dead, isn't she? Isn't she the one they found by the tracks?"

Tiffany nods.

"Well, didn't it occur to you that your subject had to be alive? And don't say I didn't say the person had to be, because I don't want to hear it. That's exactly what I mean."

"Yes, Mrs. Glaser."

Mrs. Glaser stares at the page again, clearly in some kind of pain now, which in turn gives rise to a ball of anxiety in Tiffany's chest.

"Are all these people supposed to be doing the interview with you?"

Tiffany doesn't know the answer. She was just trying to get it right, to give credit to all the people who said what they said. But this explanation seems irrelevant now, and she keeps it to herself.

"And who is this under the bridge?"

"The man?"

"The man? Well, Tiffany, does the man have a *name*, do you think? Should you maybe *say* what his name is?"

"I don't know."

And Mrs. Glaser gives her exactly the same disappointed look that every other "I dunno" she's ever heard in class has drawn. Only this is the first time it's been directed at her. She drops her eyes.

"I'm sorry, Mrs. Glaser," she mutters. "I tried, well, at first I was going to—"

But she can no more reveal this to Mrs. Glaser than she could to Mrs. Taylor.

"I mean, I was wondering, you know, if some people knew some things I could put in there."

But that's not an interview, obviously, and they both know it, so she abandons this tack as well and stands mute.

Mrs. Glaser breathes heavily for a moment, takes a red pencil out of her desk, and draws a big *F* in a circle at the top of the paper.

"If you want to be the editor," she says, "you are going to have to show me you can do a lot better than this, young lady. Do you understand me?"

"Yes, Mrs. Glaser," Tiffany says, taking the sheet of paper.

She walks down the hall with the paper in her hand. Her feet slide across the flooring she has come to love, the speckled riot of dark colors, like a multitude of stones leveled down and polished to a high gloss to transport her on her way. In eight months, she will leave it all behind for a middle school whose walls, fixtures, and floors she knows nothing about.

She pushes through the doors to the schoolyard. The grass is still green and inviting, and she walks into it, kicking at the first fallen leaves of the season. She stops and looks at the paper, at her fluid, confident handwriting, at the blazing *F*. Her first. Maybe there will be others. Maybe there will be no yearbook, no two bit imitation of the high-schoolers' effort with photocopied pages full of blurry pictures. Maybe she doesn't care.

In her pocket, her knuckle hits something hard. She takes it out to look at it. It's the tarnished silver cross she took from Denise Freeman when nobody was looking. The chain is lost, probably having come loose in the laundry that her pants have been through several times since that day. The tarnish is patterned, like the whorls of a finger pressed into the metal, and she knows this is what must have fascinated her. Her stupid habit of latching onto things, like the purple sandals and that church lady's hat, is why she picked it up. She never thought about it before, but she does now—holds her own habit out apart from herself, takes a look at it, decides she'd be better off without this peculiar tic. She clenches the cross in a fist, reels back, and throws it as far away from her as she can. But it is very light, and travels only a few yards before it drops in the grass and lies there, glinting dully back at her.

Behind the Black Curtain

Kel Walker's kitchen. There's no electricity out in Pickettsville yet, so the two men and a woman sitting at the table get by on the light of a kerosene lamp. The men, both white, are in their twenties and forties, respectively, the first slender and burr-headed, the second beefy and wispy-haired. The woman is dark-skinned and slight of build. On her head is a large, wide-brimmed black hat, beribboned and bowed, that is a good deal finer and more festive than the rest of her threadbare clothing. The men speak intimately, the woman is silent. The year is 1919.

The men conclude their discussion and shake hands, and the younger man, whose name is Gerritt, leaves. The older, whose name is Sauer, regards the woman. He tells her gruffly to remove the hat. Now that he's closed the transaction, he wants a better look than the quick glance he got earlier. The woman makes no move to obey him. He repeats the demand, more loudly. She still makes no move or acknowledgment. Next time, he strikes the table with his fist as he speaks. The woman does not flinch.

The man rises from his place, skirts the table, and reaches for the hat. Now the woman raises her head and faces Sauer. A large scar, such as might result from a heavy blow or the botched repair of a harelip, splits her upper lip into halves and pushes her nose slightly to one side. Her eyes are fish-shaped and very, very dark. She reaches up, exposing stubby fingers, and lifts the hat by its brim. Off her forehead the hat comes first, then off her crown, exposing a bulbous expanse far too large for her small hands and slender shoulders. Then, finally, her enormous head shines in the light of the lamp.

Sauer stares at it. It is covered with an elaborate, intricate maze of ridges and furrows, strange, snaking braids that worm over her oily scalp, their breadth seemingly too small for them to have been made by human hands. The patterns remind Sauer of Arabic designs he saw in Spain while traveling through Europe with his wife years ago. But he is repulsed by the oily glistening, and by the head itself, as swollen as the belly of a pregnant woman.

Sauer takes the hat from the woman's hands and pulls it back onto her head. It goes easily. He guesses, rightly, that the lining is pure silk.

He sits down again. The woman continues watching him. She moves her mouth as if she is pushing a bolus of food into her cheek, and the effect is thoroughly disgusting. And yet, Sauer cannot say that he finds the rest of his troupe appealing, or himself either, for that matter. If she is worth the finder's fee he has just paid to Gerritt for bringing her to him, he will get used to this new one. He's gotten used to the rest.

She watches him still. He takes a smoked-glass bottle from his pocket and pours two fingers of yellow whiskey into a dirty shot glass. He pushes it across the table toward the woman and tells her to drink it. He doesn't mean it to be an offer of welcome, really, but it is not exactly an order either. Whatever it is, she accepts it. She lifts the glass and downs the contents, and her face contorts from the bite of it. In a few moments she sways and falls forward, and her head hits the table with a thump.

It occurs to Sauer, only then, that the woman may not have eaten in some time. He has no idea where Gerritt found her, or in what condition. He grunts, wipes the glass with his shirttail, pours himself a shot, and swallows it. Then he drinks another. At last, adequately fortified, he takes the hat carefully off the woman's head and pulls the lamp close by.

Her name is Antoinette. A ridiculous name, a powder-puff, French name for a woman of translucent skin and smooth hair falling in waves like water. Not a name for a specimen.

He knows she will be trouble as soon as he takes her to the barn where the others sleep. Kel Walker's barn, where they are staying while they perform around Pickettsville. In the gathering dusk, unable to even see her clearly, they still recoil in fear. Louzie, the singer, dark as slate and stout as a washboard; Fleet and Crowder, Louzie's bean-headed accompanists, who swear they are not brothers; Chick, half-black and half-Italian, with his flock of trained alley cats; and Menanger, with all his poultices, powders, and tonics, who, Sauer believes, could kill a man with nothing more than some salt, ash, dirt, and a dash of his own spit.

They draw back. *This is not a freak show!* Louzie's eyes flash. Fleet and Crowder seem glued together. Only Chick regards the hat; the rest avert their eyes. He makes one of his shushing sounds and the cats, which have been curling around his legs, spring forward and surround Antoinette, who regards them silently. She is deaf and dumb, and though she reads Sauer's lips expertly in the light, seems not to have picked up the silent communications that have passed among the group.

The cats circle Antoinette's ankles, growing more agitated by the moment. Everyone knows what is happening. Chick has given them the signal for food and pointed them at a woman who has none. They hiss at her, swipe thin, bloody scratches on her legs with their claws. Finally she seems to sense what Chick has done. Her head rolls back slightly, the hat falls off, and before it hits the dirt the cats have scattered to the four corners of the barn and disappeared.

They stare at her, the globe of her head, her rigid body. She seems to be having a seizure, not one that throws her to the ground in a thrashing fit, but one that has locked her limbs and her body into some sort of spasm.

Sauer steps forward. The others make way for him. He gathers up the hat and puts his meaty hands on Antoinette's shoulders. She gurgles, jolts, and comes out of her fit. She looks at Chick, Louzie, all of them, as if she has never seen them before and so believes completely in their innocence, the lack of which they have just displayed.

"Here," Sauer says, covering her head with the hat. And he leads her toward a large pile of hay.

It is clear, in a day or so, that Antoinette is dying. She is skin and bones, she moves without energy, and she sleeps for upwards of ten hours a night. She dozes through breakfast the first two mornings she is with Sauer's troupe and nobody wakens her for her plate of hominy and sausage. Sauer throws his to the cats. Walker's sausage is all fat and gristle anyway, and it is a miracle that even they will touch it.

Around noon he nudges her haunch with the toe of his boot. Dream-dazed, she regards him stupidly for a moment, then seems to remember where she is. Then she launches into her phlegmatic cough, the other sure sign that Gerritt, that son of a bitch, has extracted money from Sauer in exchange for expiring goods.

"Get up," he says to her. "We do a show this afternoon."

She sleeps in a turban like some kind of Moslem, only hers is a cloth of fuzzy blue which, when unwound, must be the size of a tent. She knows that she must wash in the pond out back and then beg Mrs. Walker for a biscuit or something to bide her hunger. Knowing all this, she lies in the straw looking at him.

He nudges her again. "Get a move on."

She rolls away from him. He follows her, tensed. She cannot even gather herself to rise from the miserable bed of straw, and it only freshens the insult of having five perfectly good dollars stolen from him.

Menanger laughed at him over cards about it. Threw his winning hand on the barrel out back of Walker's barn where they were playing and took even more of Sauer's money. "Least she ain't no kin o' yours you gotta pay to put in the ground," Menanger opined, sweeping up the cards. "Maybe I'll buy her a nice box, you keep giving me your money."

"Deal," Sauer said dryly. For some time he had taken Menanger's jokes of this order as digs about his dead wife and son. But he figured out, eventually, that Menanger didn't even remember his wife and son. Menanger was just Menanger.

Now he follows Antoinette into the hay. The clean bristles—it amazes him sometimes, how clean, even antiseptic, fresh hay can be—rub under his boot soles. He grabs a handful of it, flings it at her, and watches it fall harmlessly around her prone form. Then he gets on one knee and reaches for her shoulder.

She rolls over again, dodging him, and lies facing him. She doesn't cringe, doesn't run away, doesn't do anything but stay just beyond his grasp. And wait. He has given Louzie a fat lip for less, but this one, this one he will be content to show who decides where she will be and when. He gets her firmly by her dress collar and gives it a good twist until his knuckles graze her head where the turban has come loose, and his fingers sink into softness where there should be none.

He leaps up, yelping, as if he has put his hand in a flame. He should be able to quell this reaction, to swallow it back, but he has to rush outside, into the weeds along the side of the barn, where he retches into the scrub and dandelions. But that is small relief. His fingers have a memory. They tingle with it, no matter what he does with his hand, and he wishes he could take a hacksaw and cut the damned thing off.

They set up in a lot behind the Meagher General Store, just off the town square. A tent, a stage, Menanger selling off the back of his wagon. It has always bugged Sauer that, no matter what entertainments he brings to the small towns they visit, it is Menanger who draws the biggest crowd and makes the most money.

This time is different. Pickettsville knows Menanger's type and his wares, but Antoinette is new to them and the tent only heightens her mystique. Sauer seats her in a kitchen chair with her back to the audience behind a thin, gauzy curtain he stole from Mrs. Walker. When the tent is full, holding about twenty people, he begins talking. What little there is of his German accent, unwanted gift from his long-dead parents, he cloaks under the singsongy cadences of a carnival hawker. Usually he takes no part in the show save to announce the stage songs and skits and take people's money, but today he finds he likes to talk.

He tells them that Antoinette is a princess from Ethiopia, expelled by her tribe for a cruel deformity resulting from a difficult birth. That, realizing their error and despairing at what they had done, the tribe begged her to return—for they had also expelled great beauty. But she left them behind, never to return to her native land. As he speaks he thinks of all manner of embellishments he might add to draw out the story, but from the expectant looks on the faces of the farmers and children standing before him, he knows that he has done enough this time.

He draws the curtain back. The people push forward, but he stops them at the curtain line. Antoinette's head glistens. The tiny braids, hundreds of them, form an impossibly complex pattern of overlapping geometries and organic shapes fused into what could almost be a kind of writing. There are gasps. The children want to touch, but Sauer need not restrain them because their parents grab them quickly. Throughout it all, Antoinette's bulbous head weaves ever so gently on the scrawny stalk of her neck.

Sauer makes the people form a line and file past the parted curtain, one by one, and out the door. When the last of them has left, thirty minutes have passed. Louzie's singing, Crowder's whacking on his tambourine, Menanger's shrill barking, all of it leaks into his ears now as if he has just removed his head from under a glass jar. When he moves, the tinkle of coins in his pockets reminds him of what he knew early on: that tomorrow's crowd will be bigger.

He goes to Antoinette. Her eyes are closed, and a momentary thrill of fear rushes through him. But then she opens her eyes. She draws a scrap of paper out of the pocket of her dress, and a pencil, and begins writing. She has a wobbly hand, but a fast one.

"Coffee," the note says. Nothing more.

He tosses it on her lap. Does she think *he* is *her* lackey?

But it is not as if she could walk over to Meagher's and buy it herself. Ethiopian princesses do not stroll around dusty southern Pennsylvania towns in big, extravagant black hats, at least not if they want to hold court in a dirty tent for five-cent admissions.

He goes and buys it for her, and boils it in a pot from Menanger's wagon.

The second day draws a crowd of fifty. Sauer must split them into two groups and make one impatient bunch stand outside for the duration of the first show. When the viewing line is almost finished, he lets his attention wander for a moment and turns back to the curtain to find Antoinette's chair empty. A triangle of light comes in through the back of the tent where a flap has been disturbed.

He finds them behind Meagher's store. Antoinette's dress is

ripped, one of her shoes is off. Two rangy, rosy-faced blond boys in overalls have her against the wall. Sauer kicks one in the small of the back, sending him writhing, and slams a shovel into the other one's ear. He tells the one who can still hear that if they try it again, neither will be fit to fuck a goat, much less a woman, when he is through with them.

Antoinette he hauls back to the tent, by way of the rear flap. He seats her. Can you finish, he asks her. She seems to be far away, as if even she is convinced of the Ethiopia hogwash and is dreaming now of grass huts and a painted husband with a spear. He pinches her cheek, hard, but she doesn't rise from her swoon.

He slips out by the flap and finds Menanger, who at first refuses to be interrupted. Then Menanger gives him a bottle to wave under her nose, instructing him to neither spill, nor allow her to drink, a single drop. When Sauer screws off the cap, the stuff nearly makes him faint. It brings Antoinette back to where, it is clear, she does not want to be. She makes a move to get up, and he pushes her back down in the chair.

"Can you finish?" he asks her again.

He has a forearm across her clavicles so that his muscles bulge just below her chin. Her stubby hands pull the torn fabric of her dress back into place. He steps back and bends down to examine her eyes. She coughs in his face.

While he is a step away, wiping his face, contemplating knocking her head off and throwing away all the money that head can make, she takes the pencil and a paper from her pocket. By some miracle, she has retained both. She begins coughing again, sending a light pink spray over the page she is writing on.

She hands him the note.

"Are you a doctor?" it says.

Perhaps it was the way he examined her eyes. He doesn't know. None of the rest of them have figured it out, assuming they even cared to guess.

He stares at her. "Tuberculosis. Epilepsy," he says. "Hydrocephalus. I can't cure you, nobody can."

Her eyes darken slightly, as if to tell him she knows all of this. And she smiles, just barely, just enough for him to see. She reaches behind the chair and releases the curtain, and it falls in place for the next show.

Slowly, surely, she insinuates herself into their affairs. When they are gearing up for shows, when they are practicing routines or inventing new ones, when they are simply hanging around Walker's place with nothing to do but needle one another, she is there, watching, making her presence familiar. Mostly they tolerate her.

But Louzie complains to Sauer that watching Antoinette dress is giving her nightmares. She insists that Antoinette sleep somewhere other than in the barn with the rest of them, but Sauer throws up his hands in a show of impotence and asks, where else? The master bedroom with Walker and his wife? In truth, he is happy to see Louzie get what she deserves. He suspects that, contrary to her agreement with him, she, Crowder, and Fleet go off on their own and perform for the Negroes out in the countryside between the official shows. Let her lose a little sleep.

Menanger predicts that Antoinette will not travel well. That when, in a week, they leave Pickettsville and head for Virginia, they will have to keep stopping to rest her from the rough ride and find her doctors when she has one of those fits that doesn't just stop on its own. It's either that or dump her off on the side of the road, which Sauer is too much of a coward to do, Menanger says, chewing on a piece of straw as he tacks the sole of one of his shoes. Sauer leaves him at his wagon without answering and walks off down the road into Pickettsville.

There, he picks up his mail. There's a letter from his brother, Ernst, suggesting for the thousandth time that he come to Muenster and join the family bank—what is left of it after the war—if he will not go back to medicine. He throws the letter away.

His real purpose in coming is to post some letters of his own. Three of them. They are to Fitch, Gambol, and Hochshauer, men he has had no communication with since his wife, Gisela, died of influenza. He has had no need. He takes no interest in saving anyone anymore, as there are always more people to save than people to save them, and the imbalance is nothing he can change. But they will be fascinated by Antoinette, Fitch and company. The only hydrocephalics they have ever seen are bug-eyed babies in pickle jars, dead at birth or not long after.

When he returns, Antoinette is with Chick, who is putting the cats through their paces. They climb up angled ladders, leap from perch to perch, hiss and bat at each other, turn somersaults in the air. They are looking better. Chick has allowed Antoinette to clean them, something Sauer always thought cats did for themselves, and to put ribbons around the necks of each of them. Even the big tom that has pissed all the wagon wheels yellow sports a gentlemanly bit of red neckwear.

Friday is a practice day for Saturday's show, which will be not in Pickettsville but in Burton, to the south.

Walker has a piece of stage off to the side of the house. What he used it for before Sauer came along, Sauer doesn't know. Nothing would surprise him, not even finding the nails from a disassembled gallows in its weathered planks. But now it is used mostly by Louzie and her crew, who set up there around midafternoon and begin to play an hour later, when Fleet is just sober enough to finger his banjo strings.

Menanger no more likes Louzie's singing than Louzie would let any of his "home remedies" pass her willing lips, but nevertheless Menanger wanders over and joins in with a howling voice. He knows all the words to all the songs, but cannot carry a tune. Louzie ignores him. Chick and Antoinette drift over from the barn and sit beneath an oak near the stage for shelter from the ferocious sun. Sauer watches them, then saunters over himself. Even on an off day, Louzie, with her gyrating hips and growling delivery, can draw a crowd anywhere.

Sauer stands a little off to the side. Is he mistaken? Louzie seems to be singing to Antoinette. But the song is some nonsense about cutting the quickening out of a man who did her wrong, delivered with all the cold menace the words imply. Antoinette seems dreamy, but her eyes follow Louzie intently. After all the complaints, could they be commiserating? Before Sauer can figure it out, Louzie is on to another number, this one full of jokes about jelly and butter.

Later, Antoinette comes to him without his seeing her approach. Sauer nearly leaps out of his skin when she grasps his shoulder. It is the first time she has touched him, rather than the other way around, and her grip is so strong he thinks Menanger has sneaked up behind him.

"What?" he snaps.

On the kitchen table Sauer sits at, papers are sorted into piles: bills of sale, I.O.U.'s, receipts, orders. Nobody but he has the head to keep it all straight, and the least they all could do is to leave him alone to do it. But of course they do not.

Antoinette gives him a paper. On it she has written: "I have to go to Montrose. A woman there will help me."

After Burton, he tells her. He'll deal with this later.

She writes, on a new paper, one word: "Now."

He looks up at her, his eyes go to her mouth, he flinches, and he looks away again. Whatever her reasons, whatever kind of help she's going to get, it can't override his wish to see the faces of the people of Burton. Word of her will have gotten there by now. He has purchased a new curtain, black lace as fancy as the hat she wears, to place in front of her in the tent. He has whipped and teased the Ethiopian princess story into a confection even Menanger will be unable to top.

"If you leave," Sauer replies, "don't come back."

He will not trouble himself to stop her. She can wander off wherever the hell she wants. Let her try getting along, in her condition, without the guarantee of a dry place to sleep at night, a regular meal twice a day, and a way to keep both.

She takes an unsteady step backward, touches her hat, and looks around confusedly. Sauer goes back to his calculations. He hears her coughing behind him, then the scratch of her pencil again, and he finds his shoulders unaccountably growing tense with anticipation.

"Must."

That is all. One word, when she is perfectly capable of writing as many sentences as it takes to explain. Her dark eyes stare at him, seem to cloud over so that the deep black-brown of her irises fills them entirely, and he remembers another Negress, a woman bleeding to death in his hands as he tries to block her womb, through which a burly baby boy, screaming now in the arms of its father, has ripped its way into the world. So some woman in Montrose has for Antoinette a powder of newt or wing of bat to make her better. It won't, of course. It won't make a difference.

Every last one of the others will throw a fit if he allows Antoinette to skip Burton, a backwater hole full of bucktoothed farmers, while making them perform there.

He waves a hand at her and says, "Go on. Go."

Burton is a misery. Relieved of Antoinette's presence, they should unwind, relax, cruise through their performances with all the old flair. But they don't. Sauer has heard of things like this. Sometimes you cut out a tumor, and the stomach, or a lung, or the heart, collapses in on itself instead of reviving, and the bewildered patient spirals down to death.

Louzie goes half-hoarse, and two of Chick's cats mutiny in the middle of his show. He knocks one of them unconscious with a quick blow of his stick, and the audience of a few boy-men stirs itself for the first time and laughs. Menanger sits sullenly on the gate of his wagon all afternoon and sells only a few bottles of tonics.

They will straggle back to Walker's place in Pickettsville soon enough, but Sauer knows to feed them first. He rigs a spit over a fire and roasts a couple of possums. The others sit around in the dusk on rocks, overturned pails, folded bits of clothing, and watch him silently. They start to pass intermittent, offhand observations among themselves. Did you see how skinny the pigs looked? My corns are acting up. Hear it's gonna be a long, hard winter.

The same shadow of a conversation continues flitting among them as they eat. Chick's red-ribboned tom wanders into the circle and rubs at Sauer's legs. Sauer kicks it away. Chick's mangy cats have long disgusted him, and this one, flaunting a ribbon that ought to adorn a girl's dress or a lock of a woman's hair, is simply too much. The cat goes to Louzie, who hisses at it. This draws laughter. Then it comes back to Sauer. It caresses his legs until he stands, suddenly, and flings it with his boot at Menanger.

Menanger gives him a wicked grin. He waves a piece of possum flesh in front of the hungry cat.

Crowder takes out a pair of dice, rubs them in his hands, and says he's feeling lucky. He cheats brazenly at cards, but nobody knows how it is he cajoles the dice into rolling his way more often than not. They are watching his hands, looking for a clue, when Chick's cat staggers forward, gushes blood from its mouth and nose, and collapses into a twitching pile of fur. It writhes a few more times and lies still.

Chick leaps on Menanger. It is so quick, so balletic, that somebody actually gasps. But Chick is no match for Menanger, who has him on the ground, with a knee on his throat, in moments. Sauer reaches for Menanger, intending to fling him off the cat man. But he finds himself hurling Menanger against his wagon so hard that a side plank breaks and Menanger goes down in a heap. Sauer moves in and reaches for the older man's throat. His fingers close around the liver-spotted windpipe and he realizes, only then, that he is not going to let go of it by his own choice.

As it turns out, he does not have to choose. His face is suddenly full of claws, which belong not to the other cats but to Louzie, who is screaming without words in his ears.

When they arrive back at Walker's, Sauer does not let them all go into the barn. He makes Menanger sleep in his wagon and Chick on Walker's back porch. He spreads a blanket for himself in the front yard, under a pear tree, and that is where he is when he awakens early the next morning to find Antoinette floating down the road like a dream.

But she isn't floating, just moving gingerly, and she is for sure no dream, because Sauer's face stings exquisitely as soon as he is fully awake. He cannot imagine what he must look like. He climbs to his feet and hikes up his trousers.

Antoinette comes up on him gasping and coughing. Her eyes are half-closed. Whatever the woman in Montrose did for her, it has made her worse, not better. It must be the look on his face that leads her to take out a piece of paper and write him a message.

"It has been this way before. It will pass."

And he understands, finally, that she is not on the threshold of death. She is not about to expire. He leads her to a stump, tells her to sit, and kneels to put his head to her chest. If she were not so dark, he believes, she would right now be as blue as Gisela was near the end. But it will pass. He opens her mouth, sticks out his tongue to get her to mimic him; she does it, all the while following him with her dark eyes. He examines it. Her breath inexplicably eases.

He leads her into the barn and lowers her onto the hay where, black hat and all, she falls immediately into a deep and shuddering sleep—or perhaps it is another seizure. Sauer cannot tell. The rest of them, all but Menanger, come over and stand with him and gaze down at her.

Around midday Sauer decides to return to Burton. He had given up on the second show there, but now, with Antoinette back, he decides to go on with it. Nobody wants to go. He snarls at them that they are going anyway, so get ready. Only Antoinette, who has surely by now heard of the ridiculous free-for-all that ended their first day at Burton, offers no objections.

More people come this time. Church spillover mostly, Sauer guesses, plus some surplus from family visits that nobody wants to prolong. There are children to clap at Chick's cats, and women who cajole their men into buying liniments and powders from Menanger, who makes no effort to hide the purple bruise at his throat.

Antoinette can barely sit upright in her tent. Sauer must keep propping her up when she sags, and all the while she mutters a low, continuous, wet cough. She writes on a paper when he stares too long at her. "Begin."

She is telling him, now, how to run his own show? He balls up the paper and throws it into the back of the tent to show her she is not, but she simply watches him with no reaction.

He marches to the front and opens the tent, and the locals stream in. It is a smaller crowd than he anticipated, only ten or so people, and he cannot hide his disappointment from himself. As if to compensate, he launches into his story with manic energy and gestures, and in no time he has his spectators transfixed. His face contorts, spittle flies from his lips. A woman up front flinches when his loudest exclamations hit her. Finally he falls silent for a second to let them follow his pointing finger to the curtain. Then, he yanks it aside with such violence that it rips from its supports and collapses onto the dirt floor.

Antoinette has turned in the chair and rested her forehead on her wrist, which in turn rests on the chair's ladder back. Her face is hidden. The crowd, oddly, makes no sound at all as it creeps closer for a clear look at her. Then gasps of surprise rise from them. Gone are the strange geometric-organic shapes Sauer has grown accustomed to. It takes him a moment to figure out what the winding black threads reveal to him, and he pushes one of the bumpkins out of his way to get a better look. Continents and islands. He is looking at the countries of the globe. The detail is astounding, the proportions refined. The trip to Montrose was not for Antoinette's health at all.

"How do she do that?" a woman with a burnished face and gingham dress asks.

Sauer casts around for a lie, but none comes to him. He says that it is a secret, but she continues to pin him with her unsatisfied stare until he moves away.

Again he makes a viewing line, which moves slowly. The people stand staring long past the time it takes for them to make out what few lands they remember from their paltry schooling. Eventually the last of them leaves and Sauer peeks out of the tent to see how many more are waiting. There are another fifteen or so. He decides to charge them more.

He goes back to Antoinette. She remains as she has been, with her head down.

"That was good," he says.

Her head jostles, lists back and forth on her wrist a little bit. He hears a scrap of paper rustle. Her right arm, the free one, moves in the shadow of her bent form, out of his sight. She hands up a message to him.

"Help me, Dr. Sauer."

At first, he is angry. Hasn't he already told her there is nothing he can do, nothing anybody can do, to stop the ravages of her disease? But she is not likely to have forgotten this, he decides. He reads the note again, puzzling over it. Does she want the sort of help the woman in Montrose gave her? This is unlikely too. And she would not need such assistance so soon after her last visit to Montrose anyway. He reads the note for a third time, and as if it suddenly says something new, his hand falls slowly to his side.

He looks down at her, and a long, deep shudder runs the entire length of her body. With great effort, she heaves her enormous head up from the ladder back and sits rigidly upright in the chair. She stares right into his face, and he knows he has not mistaken her meaning.

In her eyes, impatience. She turns in the chair so her back is to him. He raises his hands, examines the hairy backs of them, their whiteness, and wonders what acts they are capable of. After Burton, he no longer knows. After Gisela, he had thought that he no longer cared. His confusion threatens to arrest him there, like a statue. But when Antoinette allows her head to tilt back, exposing her neck, his hands come up to meet it. This time, the softness does not make him bolt.

A Place between Stations

When we emerge from the underground tunnels of Grand Central, the late-day sky hangs above, watery and blue. Our Metro North train crosses the Harlem River and crawls, rocking, into the Bronx, where we move past brick warehouses, alarm companies, produce outfits, a stray dog in the street. The scant light from a hidden sun wipes color from the chipping signs and the cars parked tightly at the curb, muting the world framed by my window. I settle back for the long ride home.

Around me sit the others, businessmen, most of them. In polished oxfords and finely tailored wool coats, they bend their heads over the *Times*, the *Post*, or paperwork in briefcases spread open on their laps. When we pull into their stops, they will march out and thrust their keys into door locks, fire their engines. I go more slowly. Each night I reacquaint myself with the big, black BMW waiting for me in the New Haven garage. We enjoy a small courtship, my car and I, as I stroke its fenders, drink in its details. Most nights, I am the last from my train to drive away.

Behind me, the conductor moves up the aisle, punctuating his easy chat with the passengers with calls for tickets. The *cha-chunk* of his hole puncher grows louder as he draws near. I wait with my wallet in my hand and wonder whether I will find my wife, Selma, at home when I arrive. We argued last night. We have always argued, throughout the twenty-nine years of our marriage: about having children, then about raising them, about whether to live among other blacks or among whites who shared our affluence, about my unfocused ambition, the elections last fall, my leaving my socks on the bathroom floor, in Selma's words, "like a country nigger." But last night was different. Selma came out of the bathroom as I sat reading reports in bed and showed herself to me. She had removed every speck of makeup but not yet put on her night cream. I hadn't seen her this way in twenty years, and looking at her face, its usual café-au-lait foundation scoured away to reveal its true tapioca shade, I knew the point of her nakedness. She'd told me she wanted me to leave my distant job in the city. Our sons were on their own. At my age, I would rise no further in my company. These were times we should spend together, yet she passed her days alone in our big suburban house. Now she meant for me to know that she was more than just lonely; she was bereft. A woman who had drifted away from the friends of her youth and sent off her sons, who had few surviving relatives, who, though long married, lacked even a husband. As much as this stung me, I knew she was right. But instead of answering her charge, I went back to reading my reports. It was not that I no longer loved her or was seeing another woman. Nothing like that. But my work was familiar, at least, and I did it carefully, I might even say well. And I could not imagine, after all these years of commuting, a weekday that did not unwind in a long evening ride on the 4:13 train from New York City.

As the train streaks through the Botanical Gardens station, running express from 125th Street to Stamford, the conductor reaches my seat. He's a slim fellow past the age when his sandy hair should have gone gray; a slight paunch, the kind that comes of slack muscles, causes the pants of his navy uniform to droop at the waist. When he smiles, the smile spreads slowly and deeply across his flat, round face. We've never exchanged more than a ticket, on my part, and a thank-you on his. I hold open my wallet to show him my monthly pass.

"Missing something there," he tells me.

I look at the clear plastic holder and see it is empty.

The conductor winks at me. "Catch you on the way back."

With that he goes on, leaving me to fumble through my pockets and briefcase for the pass. But this is pointless; I never remove it from my wallet. For a bitter second I wonder whether Selma has taken it, but I quickly dismiss the idea because I had the pass for the morning ride. After one thorough search I give up, determined not to waste half my ride hunting a slip of paper. I'll buy a one-way ticket when the conductor returns.

The train slows and cruises through the station at Rye.

The way to see from the windows of a train: do not stare. Staring at the landscape, watching the dry cleaners and the shining new apartment complexes and the back yards of houses near the tracks, will show you the same view time and again, and after a while you look without seeing. The chance of a dialogue between you and the landscape is lost. What you must do is spend most of the ride reading, but not too deeply, or scanning the faces of the other passengers, but not too closely. Then, when you are inclined to take a break, look out the window. The view leaps at you like a sudden insight; you must grasp it quickly. You see an alley between two buildings at the end of which lies a slice of street, where an orange sign, a perfect circle, marks one weathered storefront as Alligator's Records. You remember your favorite 45, the lay of the cursive silver letters on the black label, the line that repeated because you scratched the record taking it to a party. You held it inside your coat. The vinyl felt like a wave-polished shell under your anxious fingers. The wind, as you crossed empty streets, cut at your skin where your collar and cuffs gave entry, but it couldn't harm you. Not that day. The record store blinks away.

The conductor appears again, but he is in a hurry and scoots by without stopping or catching my eye. "Keep it down, fellas," he chides a group of boys in the back of the car. The door clunks shut and he's gone.

When I look up tonight, I see houses. We have left New York and crossed into Connecticut, but the homes here are neat and modest, not the sprawling estates of Westport or Greenwich. On the upstairs floor of a shingled house, a woman steps up to the window as if to watch the train and then turns her face away suddenly as we pass. With dusk falling and the light of the room behind her she is only a silhouette, but even so the gesture moves me to avert my eyes. Selma detests my small considerations of strangers. When she catches me nodding at the panhandlers she ignores, or opening doors for women I don't know, she says nothing, but holds herself tall and aloof. She is doing it for the both of us. She is compensating for what she believes is a weakness in her husband that, even in this day and age, a black man still cannot afford. And she may be right. But at this stage of my life I feel not so much black or male, middle-aged or well-to-do or professional, as incomplete. I am son to my father, father to my boys, husband to my unhappy wife, but somehow more lost than found in the mix.

Outside, I catch a glimpse of a small pond. It lies on the grounds of a one-story house in a tangle of young maples and sumacs and scrub, and reflects the roseate glow of the horizon. Such ponds are oddities. They are the property of the landowner, but how can a body of water belong to anyone? With the snows and the rains, the water comes and goes, streaming through the land and the air in a constant motion of replacement. And so it is, many people think, with the little cemeteries that you see sometimes from the train, or out along rural highways. Fences surround them, but the fences are rusted and tumbled, and the bodies laid in the graves, having long ago turned to powder, seem ready to give up their memories freely to any who wish to take them. So the sketchers move in with their pads and the gravestone rubbers take impressions, believing that with their pencils and paper they can capture something of value.

Near the end of my youth my father took me to such a burial ground at the edge of a wood. He borrowed a friend's car and drove us thirty minutes into the countryside, away from our home in Hartford, keeping as silent along the way as was his custom. When he parked the car and led me into a grassy field, I marveled at how easily he, a city man for as long as I'd known him, covered ground that left me stumbling. He was tall and lanky, coal-dark and ashy-knuckled, a man with hard black eyes who never went outdoors without his battered cap or some other covering for his head. We went down a rise and came up on the little group of slender headstones.

They had once been white, but time had grayed them and worn away the lettering. A few had cracked in half, and the tops lay on the ground or were gone. I looked at my father. He stared down at a pair of stones at his feet. He said nothing, hinted nothing with his expression, made no motion or sign. At the time, I thought him a block of a man, and hid my embarrassment of him in the jokes I made about him with my friends and in mockery of him when his back was turned. Deep into autumn, the trees around us were bare and the grass a dead brown. I rolled my eyes upward and let my head loll back in a gesture of boredom. When I looked my father's way again, he was reaching for me. His hand clamped onto the back of my neck and forced me to my knees. The wet chill of the ground came almost instantly through my pants. He pushed harder, until my face was down at the level of the stones. But I could not read a word. Were these his parents, of whom he had said nothing to me, or his grandparents, an aunt and uncle, siblings of his I'd never known? All that he told me was in the weight of his hand. He grunted, or cleared his throat, and I thought he would speak. But instead he let me go. He immediately strode away, back toward the car. We never returned or spoke of that day again.

The train slows and pulls into the station at Stamford. Plywood walls block the view of the city. More construction. When the doors snap open, people exit in a whoosh, and a few passengers struggle against the tide to get on the train. After we've left the station, the conductor comes by, taking tickets, and I offer him the fare from New York to New Haven. He hesitates a moment, as if he hasn't considered the possibility that I might not find the pass. His face puckers oddly.

"Hold on to that," he says. "Take another look. I bet you've got that pass somewhere."

Before I can protest, he goes on to the next seats. He is starting to be the distraction that I refused to let the lost pass become. I pick up my newspaper and read with a fierce attention. The conductor doesn't interrupt me through the next several stops, but I have lost my focus, and instead of looking out the window I think of Selma.

I smelled the breakfast she cooked this morning even before I came downstairs. In place of the usual black coffee and cold, low-fat muffins, there was buttered toast, fried bacon, and eggs seared in the leftover grease. Selma was already eating when I entered our dining room. The windows look out over a terraced lawn that drops a level and gives way to woods. In the spring, cardinals and jays flit among the trees. Selma was shoveling eggs into her mouth, pushing them onto her fork with her toast.

"Get yourself a plate," she said to me.

"Selma, what about—"

"I'm eating," she interrupted. "Just eat."

I did as she ordered. The wrinkled bacon was thick-cut and salty enough to make me wince at my first bite. Charred bits of it flecked the scrambled eggs. I ate carefully at first, thinking of cholesterol and heart attacks, but then with relish. I wiped my plate with the last piece of toast.

Thinking she meant all of it as a peace offering, I began to apologize for the night before. She cut me off by standing and beginning to clear the table.

"I was going through my things this morning," she said.

I slumped back in my chair.

"When we moved from Port Chester, that hideous apartment, I threw almost all of the old things away. Except for a few. I found something I want you to have. I put it in your briefcase."

I watched as she carried the plates to the kitchen, where she dumped them all in the sink. Silverware clattered against china and glass. Selma wiped her hands and walked away.

When we reach the outskirts of Bridgeport, the twilight colors in the sky have merged and darkened. Blocks of cramped houses and low-income projects alternate with warehouses and shells of factories. Streetlights twinkle with an irreverent merriness. The Jenkins Valve Company, long since closed, looms up as the train draws near the station. There is not much left of it: three empty floors in red brick with the Jenkins name in tall, white letters across the facade. The train coasts on and pulls into Bridgeport station.

A crowd sorts itself out on the platform and streams through the open doors. A black woman my age, perhaps a bit younger, squeezes her hips and several tote bags into the seat beside me. Along with a generously cut winter coat, she wears a lavender hat like an overturned bowl fringed in black lace. Among the drab businessmen, it looks out of place, but she seems unaware. Though I have avoided catching her eye and pore conspicuously over my newspaper, she leans over, once she has gotten settled, and asks me the time.

"My son be getting home about now," she says when I tell her. "He's a lawyer. I do hope he remembers what day it is."

I nod politely.

She smiles to herself, and the crinkling of her face lights up her hazel eyes. "Baby's going to be baptized," she announces.

"That's nice," I say.

We have moved from downtown into a crumbling neighborhood. On a corner outside a bar, four men huddle around the raised hood of a dilapidated VW van.

"My first grandchild," the woman says.

"Really."

"I have a daughter, too. She lives in California."

"That's a long way."

The woman bites her lip. "Yes."

Though I meant nothing by the comment, she falls silent and arranges the straps on her tote bags. Selma's and my two sons live at a distance too. Both of them are in Dallas, Texas. Evan Jr., the oldest, calls Selma once a month and tells her anecdotes he's gathered during the office visits of his patients. He's a pediatrician. Raymond, the youngest, has no telephone. Now and then he sends postcards, as if he was constantly en route from one place to another. He last visited us eight years ago to tell us he was dropping out of Princeton.

Selma had a fit about that. She called Ray a disgrace, railed at him for having wasted our money, held up the example of his brother in medical school and asked what was wrong with him. Hadn't we given him every advantage? Hadn't we stood behind him all the way? Yes, he said. Selma raised her fists in frustration and stalked out of the room.

"Aren't you going to chew me out too?" Ray said, sliding deeper into the couch.

"Of course not," I said. "That's your mother's job."

He smiled weakly.

"I'm such a fuckup," Ray said. "I don't belong in this family. Dad, haven't you ever screwed up anything in your whole life?"

This was one of those times that I imagined many fathers took their sons aside and told them a story, one that threw a piercing light on the problem that was knotting up their boys' lives. And the stories strengthened the young men. It didn't always work; not every boy really wanted to be saved, not every father cared enough to bother. But I had no stories for Ray. The fragments I harbored would do him more harm than good.

In the seat next to me, the woman going to her granddaughter's baptism opens one of her tote bags.

"Like a candy?" she asks.

I take the foil-wrapped bonbon she offers and slip it into my pocket for Selma. I like candy well enough, but this is a habit I've developed, squirreling away all the sweets that come my way for my wife. What will I do if she is not there to take it? Then I remember that she has also given something to me, the thing she chose not to name, which she put in my briefcase. But I won't have room to open my briefcase until the woman with all her tote bags gets off.

"For after dinner," I say.

The woman nods, satisfied.

"She went out there for an operation, my daughter. That was eighty-five, eighty-six, around then. It was that surgery where they staple part of your stomach up. She was three hundred pounds."

At first I don't know what to say. "Did it work?" I finally ask.

"She's barely a hundred pounds now," the woman replies.

Her tote bag still lies open on her lap. Inside are more of the candies, wrapped in their red and blue foils, amid a tumble of brightly papered and bowed boxes.

The train wheels squeal as the cars round a bend. The pedestrians in Bridgeport's streets are turning to shadows, and headlights flash at corners. Crumbling buildings mark almost every block. I would like to step out and wander through the streets of Bridgeport tonight. It stretches on so far, reclines in a rubble of brick and glass and loose tires and twisted fences with such a presence that I lose my taste for everything smooth and pretty. This moment is a gift I would like to give to Raymond, my son. But he is far from here, it is little to offer, and I am many years too late.

A Place between Stations

We are running behind schedule this evening. When I awake from a doze and check my watch, I realize we should have arrived in New Haven by now, but we are at a place between stations that I don't recognize. The seat beside me is empty. Most of the passengers have left the train. I open my briefcase and find nothing unusual among the papers in the main compartment, nor in the flaps on the inner walls. I sift through the papers again, and this time discover an unsealed, six-by-nine manila envelope with no markings on the outside. I slide my hand in and pull out a small photograph.

Its leather frame is so cracked, so grayed, it might be stone. The photo is one of myself at eight, perhaps ten years of age. I don't remember having seen it before. How Selma may have come by it, I have no idea. Both of my parents were dead by the time we married, and she'd been in contact with nobody else in my family. I peer at it closely. The fat lips and cheeks, the narrow head with its tuft of hair at the center, the close-set eyes looking up and away, all of the features are so unlike mine now and yet, in that face, I can see traces of the self I know. Selma. My wife keeps no scrapbooks or boxes of mementos. Each spring, she dons a white apron when the neighbors are tending their daffodils and sweeps away what little debris we have accumulated in the year past. Yet she has kept him with her all this time, all these years, harbored this boy-self I would have thought she would have no use for. Slowly, I shut my briefcase. I look around for the conductor to ask him when we will arrive, but he is nowhere to be found.

Then the train brakes. I grab my coat, my newspaper, and my briefcase. As we come into the station I watch a concrete platform appear, then a yellow warning strip, posters for Broadway shows and computers. But the stop is unfamiliar, and its name does not slide into view. Beyond the lighted platform, it is too dark to make out any landmarks. I wait for the announcement of the station. The doors snap open. Finally the conductor's voice crackles over the loudspeakers and says, in relaxed tones, "Don't forget to check the overhead rack and the seats around you for personal belongings. Watch your step leaving the train. And hurry home. It's cold out there."

ABOUT THE AUTHOR

Photo by Kurt Keefner

Stephanie Allen is Lecturer in the Department of English at the University of Maryland in College Park. She holds a B.A. from Yale University and an M.F.A. from the University of Maryland. She received a Maryland State Arts Council Individual Artist Award in 2002, and was a finalist in the 2001 Associated Writing Programs Award Series in Short Fiction. Ms. Allen lives with her husband in Greenbelt, Maryland.